Robin's Country

ROBIN'S COUNTRY

MONICA FURLONG

A TRUMPET CLUB SPECIAL EDITION

ISBN 0-590-98123-4

Copyright © 1995 by Monica Furlong. Cover illustration copyright © 1995 by Neal McPheeters. All rights reserved. Published by Scholastic Inc., 555 Broadway, New York, NY 10012, by arrangement with Alfred A. Knopf, Inc. TRUMPET and the TRUMPET logo are registered trademarks of Scholastic Inc.

12 11 10 9 8 7 6 5 4 3 2   6 7 8 9/9 0 1/0

Printed in the U.S.A.

Spring

ONE

Dummy

ALTHOUGH IT WAS APRIL it was cold in the barn, and the cold made him wheeze. He covered his legs and the rest of his body with hay as much as he could, and with just his arms outside the cocoon he ate very slowly the slice of bread he had saved, enjoying every crumb. The crust was especially delicious. He was tired, but knew he wouldn't sleep quickly. He hated being shut up on these light evenings, because it was more difficult to go to sleep. It had been a bad day, with Master quick with his fists, and Mistress in a temper, which meant that he got less to eat than usual, not much more than a salt herring. In spite of the bread he was terribly hungry now, and that made the spring cold harder to bear. He lay very still in the hay, trying to think of something that would comfort him.

It had been a hard day, too, because of Master's son, Roger. Roger and his friends had pelted him with mud and stones when he was alone with the sheep, and Roger had pulled him by the ear and half thrown him against the thorn hedge. His ear still hurt—he explored it gently—and the thorns had torn his ragged trousers and scratched his skin. He spent a few enjoyable minutes thinking of terrible forms of revenge he might take against Roger, but then sighed as he came back to reality. He was far too small and skinny to fight Roger, let alone win the battle.

Then he spent a few minutes working on his running-away plan. He would need to run at night because Master and Mistress never let him out from under their eye all day, and his problem would be to take enough food to keep him going longer than a few hours. Somewhere, out in that world, he thought there must be kind people who would take care of him. Even though it was a long time since he had met anyone like that, he remembered that there were such people, who talked in gentle voices and smiled at you and didn't hit you all the time. But it might take several days to find them, so he would need enough food to keep going. Then again, he did not walk all that fast, and he was afraid that a horse could soon catch up with him. Master and he had sometimes passed the Forest—deep green and full of lovely shadows—but he knew that wolves and robbers roamed all over it, so it would be no good to escape that way. He would simply get eaten alive or hung from a tree.

After a bit he remembered that he knew something that comforted him more than either revenge or daydreams, even though he didn't really understand it. He had puzzled over it a lot without getting any further. He shook the hay from his arms, and pushed it away from around him until the earth floor was clear. Then, enjoying every moment, he reached behind the tack for his secret stick that he had carefully sharpened, and began to use the point on the bare floor. The first thing to do, he remembered, was to scratch a straight upright line with a circle on one side of it, itself propped up by a smaller line as by a crutch. Then he had to inscribe a straight line, without adornments this time. Next, a curled shape open at one side. (Many years ago, when the woman with fair hair had taught him in that comfortable room beside the fire, he had thought it was like a hedge they had in the garden that kept the wind off you.) Then two upright sticks with a line stretching between them. Then a sort of tent. Then the same shape as the first one, only his arm was getting a bit sore now and he did not get it quite right. Then another curved shape, but closed on one side.

His task done, he looked at the scratched shapes with pleasure, and a warm feeling inside. They reminded him of Her; when She put out a hand it was not to cuff him or pull his hair, but to caress him. He had sat close beside Her with a wax tablet and a silver thing in his hand—it was much easier to scratch the wax than the beaten earth of Farmer Jordan's floor. He thought—he wasn't sure—that perhaps he had sometimes scratched other things on the wax tablet. What could they have meant? What did this scratching mean except that it was something important to do with himself that She had said he must never, never forget. He had kept his promise.

"Where's Dummy?" The voice that he dreaded above all voices broke into his memory. So swiftly that there seemed no moment between the thought and the deed, he covered the floor with hay and lay down on his side, pulling the hay over himself, pretending to be asleep.

"In the barn."

The door of the barn screamed open, Master's boots came heavily over the floor, and a painful kick landed on his bottom.

"Get up."

He opened his eyes, startled as if he really had been asleep, and stared up, frozen with uncertainty, into the angry face. Master bent down, and in one movement scooped up his thin body. Half carrying him, half dragging him by the scruff of his neck, he pulled him out of the barn, across the yard, and into the kitchen. Roger looked up from his warm seat by the fire, gleeful at the spectacle.

Mistress was kneading bread, thumping the dough angrily as if she wished she was thumping him. "You've got it coming to you this time," she said. "Serves you right."

He had no idea what he had done, but he was pretty sure what the consequences were going to be, as he watched Master take off his belt. The cat, who had been sitting by the fire, dashed behind a chair, and he wished he could do the same.

Master always gave you a talking-to before he hit you, so he would soon know what he was supposed to have done. Probably he was going to be punished because he had stolen food—he was always stealing food because otherwise the pain inside him got too great to be borne. He had long ago decided that it was worth an occasional beating. But no, Master was talking about a knife that he had taken. He had looked at it that morning, that was for sure—it had had such a beautiful hasp that he could not take his eyes off it, and he had admired the bright shining blade. Mistress had seen him looking and had boxed his ears. But there it was on the table, the blade chipped and blunted, the bright colors of the hasp dimmed. Then suddenly he remembered that when he met Roger and his friends down by the brook Roger had hidden something from him before he started to throw stones. Yes, and something had slipped from his pocket and fallen into the brook. He himself could not stop to find out what it was, but now he guessed that Roger had been showing off to his friends, had damaged the knife and rescued it, with its colors dimmed, from the brook. Now *he*, Dummy, was to get the blame for it.

He tried not to cry, although Master hurt him a lot, because he had long ago taught himself to behave with pride—"like a king," he told himself—

whatever they did. The belt stung his back until it felt as if a flame was being held to his body. It took Master a long time—Roger kept urging him on— but even though Dummy was white and faint and trembling when Master put his belt back on he stood up as tall as he could, and almost unconsciously his lip curled with contempt as he looked at Master. Only then the floor started to move unpleasantly and his legs seemed to be rooted there, and he thought maybe he would be sick.

Later, he came around to Mistress's saying, "Maybe you overdid it, Jack. The kid's not strong." She held a tumbler of water to Dummy's lips and he drank thirstily, but his head still buzzed and swam.

"You go to bed," said Mistress to her husband. "I'll just finish my bread and I'll follow you up."

Master and Roger made their way to bed, leaving Mistress and Dummy together. Mistress had never shown him any kindness and he did not expect it now, so he was taken aback when she said, "You'd better stay in here for tonight, Dummy. You look poorly." He had often looked poorly before, he thought, and she hadn't seemed to care. Maybe she really did think Master had gone too far.

"Here," she said. "Here's a cup of milk for you." She lifted an old blanket off the settle, the one she threw around her shoulders in winter when she went out to feed the hens. Dummy drank the warm, rich liquid gratefully, and huddled himself into the blanket, longing for sleep.

TWO

Running Away

AN HOUR OR TWO PASSED in which Dummy was not aware of very much except the warmth of the fire on his body, the pain in his back, the rich comfort of the milk. His ragged shirt, stained with blood, had stuck to his back. In an awkward position, because it hurt too much to lie down, he dozed, but woke before long, feeling he had something that he needed to think about urgently. Tomorrow would not do.

Earlier in the evening—weeks ago, it seemed—he had dreamed of getting away from this hateful place where they worked him to death and beat him for things he had not done. He had thought that he must creep away at night, but usually he was locked in the barn and could not go anywhere. Tonight, however, he was not locked in. Nor was he short of food. There were three loaves of bread, still warm, on the table; cold meat hung in the larder, and there was a huge pitcher of milk. The temptation to take big bites out of the bread was so great that it was difficult to think clearly. Yet thinking was important and drew him to one certain conclusion. He broke out in a sweat as he realized what he intended to do, and for a few moments was so frightened that he almost decided to stay where he was, enjoying the unusual treat of the warmth all night long.

Yet he knew that if he proposed to run away this was the best time of year. The summer was coming on. If he found himself forced to sleep in the countryside, or in the streets and alleyways of a big town, he would not freeze to death. He still hesitated, but then he remembered how ill he had been the previous winter and how he had thought that if he had to live through another winter like that one, he might die. He had nothing to lose by going.

Quiet as he could be, he began to creep about the room, making preparations. He took Master's wool shirt as it dried near the fire, thinking it would make an ample smock to go over his rags, which it did. He had no proper shoes, but he found socks and over them bound strips of leather that Master used around his legs in the wet. He took up Mistress's small basket—not the big one she took to market— and in it placed a herring, a bit of salt pork, a flask of milk, and one of the warm loaves of dark bread. The basket was then so heavy he dared not put any more into it, though he snatched generous mouthfuls of bread and drank more milk. The fact that he felt very guilty about taking it did not lessen his hunger. He arranged the rough blanket warmly around his shoulders.

He was ready to go. He dared not open the kitchen door, which he knew, from past experience, gave a warning screech. The larder had a tiny door through which they dragged in carcasses from the cart to save shouldering them around the yard. Because he was so small he could slither through the low hole, though the touch of the wood on his sore back made him want to cry out. Once out in the yard he waited a moment, wondering if Mistress had heard, but all was silent. He put his head around the door of the barn and took his sharpened stick. He looked wistfully at the big cart horses, but he was too small to ride them, and Master would have woken at the sound of one of them clattering out of the gate. Many years ago in that other life he had ridden a pony, a pretty dark creature with a white star on its forehead. He said a long good-bye to Noble, his favorite among Master's horses, who had comforted many a lonely night with his warm breath and sturdy presence. The cocks were not crowing yet. He had two or three hours before the hue and cry would be after him. Suddenly it seemed very little time.

HE WALKED NERVOUSLY through Ollerton, the local village, and out of it on the other side, hoping nobody would look out from the silent cottages. The basket rubbed painfully on his shoulder, and the leathers did not feel good under his feet, but, after a mile or two, somehow these pains faded, and all that mattered was to keep going, mile after mile, to get away from the farm as fast as his legs could take him. He broke off more of the bread and ate it as he walked along, and it cheered him at once. He was shocked at how trembly he was, how slowly he walked, and, increasingly, how tired he felt.

The sun came up like a ball tossing on a bank of palest green. There was something so joyful about it, it comforted him. He walked on, enjoying the warmth as the sun rose higher. Soon, he knew, he would have to sit down for a bit. He wandered quite a long way into a wood and propped himself against a tree and ate some more of his delicious food. It was the best food he had had in months, yet somehow he was not as hungry as he would have expected. His throat hurt and he felt rather hot. He dozed. Or at least he intended to doze. When he eventually woke he suspected that he had slept for longer than he had intended. He cursed himself, the more so since, when he got out on the road again, his whole body seemed to hurt, his head ached, and his footsteps dragged. But he kept on, step after step. Soon he reached a bleak heathland and realized to his dismay that if Master came to look for him here there would be no cover for him. Away in the distance, it was true, there were trees, many trees, but here there was nothing but gorse and low shrubs. Nowhere for even a small boy to hide.

Although by now it was agony to swallow, and he longed to lie down and go to sleep again more than anything in the world, he set his teeth, fixed his eyes on the distant trees, and kept going toward them. Sometimes they swam before his eyes in a sort of haze, sometimes he could see them quite clearly. Inside his head he kept saying, "Trees . . . trees . . . trees." He even made it into a rhythm to walk to and it made him go faster. "Trees and trees and trees and trees . . ."

Finally, almost sobbing with relief, he reached the first of the trees and saw that they stretched away for miles. It was then that he heard the sound of hooves, coming fast along the road he had just traveled. It seemed to him that he knew perfectly well whose horses those were—Master's and Roger's—and that, to his surprise, he knew what to do. With what strength he had left he pulled himself up into one of the oak trees already covered in leaves, and found that it made a perfect hiding place. He dragged his basket with him. He could see nothing of the ground except the tiny bit at the foot of the trunk, and this comforted him, since it meant that others could not see him.

The hooves came nearer and stopped, and the voices he knew so well discussed him.

"He'd never go into Sherwood Forest. It's too dangerous and he knows it." (Dummy knew that, for some reason, Master was afraid of the Forest and the people who lived in it.) "If he's headed for Worksop he must be somewhere along this road, either farther on or we've passed him in hiding somewhere on the way. If we keep on this road tonight, Ben and Tib patrol the road to Newark like I told 'em, and Ned rides out to Mansfield, we're bound to catch the little villain."

"I bet he'll be sorry when you do, Dad."

"He'll wish he'd never been born. I'll teach him to run off."

Just then Dummy looked down and was shocked to see that part of the loaf of bread must have tumbled out of the basket and was lying at the foot of the tree. *Oh, God, please don't let them notice.*

They didn't notice. Roger returned along the road he had traveled, and Master set off along the road ahead of Dummy.

When they had gone, Dummy gradually ceased to tremble. What was he to do? If he walked along the road they would trap him, but this wood, these friendly trees, were the terrible Forest of which he had often heard, full of wolves and robbers.

Perhaps because by now he was beginning to have a fever, an unusually vivid picture formed in his mind. It was a picture of, well, a sort of house, but not like an ordinary house, or at least not like the ones in Ollerton. It had a tall woman in it and a handsome, brown-haired man, and they smiled at each other in the way that he remembered people doing from long ago. He had got it into his head that this magical place was on the other side of the Forest or that, at any rate, all he had to do was to walk boldly into the Forest to find it. The wolves or the robbers might get him first, he knew, but he felt now that that might be no worse than being caught by Master or Roger.

He eased his sore, bruised, aching body down from the tree, settled his basket onto his shoulder, and walked as quickly as he could away from the road, toward the green heart of the Forest.

Not looking to right or left for fear of what he might see, Dummy walked and walked, his feet hurting like fire, his legs growing heavier and more unwilling. He knew his strength was failing. Always a weakling—so Master complained—the combination of the beating he had received and whatever else was the matter with him made it seem impossible to go on. His throat hurt dreadfully, his head was pounding. It was obvious that he would not get to the other side of the Forest before nightfall, but this meant that he would almost certainly be eaten by the wolves. Already, he thought, shadows lurked ominously among the trees.

He sank down beside a large oak tree, its mossy roots forming a kind of seat. He closed his eyes, but his inner world was full of brilliant whirling shapes that bewildered him. He leaned back against the trunk, his eyes open now to drive away the shapes, and watched the last of the daylight disappear. Somewhere, perhaps as he climbed down from the tree, he had lost his blanket, and he now felt bitterly cold. His teeth began to chatter. He dozed for a while until he was startled wide awake by the sound of human voices. Glancing backward among the trees he thought that, a long way away, he could see lanterns. Was this part of his sickness? No, because he could also hear men shouting to one another. He guessed that Master had roused a search party to find him.

Weariness and pain forgotten, he stood up and began to run as fast as he could, away from the shimmering lights. The lights were left far behind but still Dummy ran, stumbling over roots, scratching himself on bushes, running, running. His breath came in terrible, sharp wheezes, and his chest hurt so much that he thought he would burst, yet he dared not stop. On and on he went, sobbing as he ran, caring for nothing but to avoid his pursuers. All the misery of the past few years seemed to be chasing him.

He was by now so blind to everything about him that he did not notice when he ran into a clearing, deep in the heart of the Forest, and toiled up a slope on the far side of it. It was set with huge rocks, and Dummy scrambled desperately among them, lost, terrified. He found what seemed to be a rough path that wound upward. There was a dark patch, and on the far side of it a smooth grassy sward illuminated by the moon. Racing to reach the sward, Dummy fell. He did not simply fall over, as he had expected, but he fell downward, feet first, and to his horror seemed to be slithering fast down a tunnel or hole. He tried to clutch with his hands, or obtain a hold with his feet, but he was going too fast for that. The tunnel curved sharply, and with a gasp Dummy shot out into what appeared to be a room or a cave, which, to his amazement, was full of light and people. He was blinded after the darkness outside and terrified that somehow he had fallen among a gang of robbers. Lying dazed after his long fall he still put up a hand to protect his face from a blow. He tried to stand up, to see where he was, to save himself from whatever fate was about to inflict on him, but as he staggered to his feet nausea overwhelmed him, and he pitched over and fell.

THREE

Outlaws!

EMERGING FROM THE BLACKNESS Dummy could not think where, or even who, he was. His eyes took in a face framed in dark curly hair and another plump face beyond. He seemed to be lying in a cave lit by candles, with a big fire in the center of it.

"Are you feeling better?" asked the face with the curly hair, and he was surprised to hear that the voice was a woman's, although the head with its short hair looked like that of a boy. He was expecting anger, but her voice sounded cool, though not particularly friendly. He was conscious that she was watching him closely. She produced a goblet with water in it, and he took it from her and drank greedily. He tried to pull himself up into a sitting position, but immediately the cave swam around in the most horrible way, and he sank back again weakly.

"You've had a long journey!" the woman commented. She got up and moved across the cave, filling a bowl from a huge pitcher, picking up a cloth and a comb. He was astonished to see that she wore leather leggings, and a leather tunic like a man's. She *couldn't* be a woman, and yet she appeared to be one.

Back at his side, she dipped the cloth in the water and bathed his face and neck and hands. His smock was covered in blood and mud, and she looked at it doubtfully.

"Would you like to take it off?" she asked. "I could find you a clean one." Without waiting for his reply, she began easing it over his head, until he sat in his ragged shirt. When she saw the bloodstains on the back of it, however, she exclaimed, "Who beat you?" This time she paused a moment for his answer and seemed puzzled not to receive it.

Removing the shirt was painful to him, but she did the difficult work quite gently. Then she bathed his back. Again she crossed the room, this time to fetch a jar of salve. "This will hurt as I put it on, but it should help a bit," she said.

It did hurt too—the tears came into his eyes, though he winked them away—but he could feel the puckered skin smoothing under the ointment. The woman put a piece of soft cloth on his back and anchored it with a bandage. Then she gave him a linen shirt—"Rather big for you, I'm afraid"—and a clean smock, and turned to unwrap his feet, which were a nasty, bloodstained sight.

"Where have you come from?" she asked him.

When once more he did not speak, her eyes searched his.

Meanwhile, the other occupant of the cave, a very plump man who wore a brown monkish robe, was making a rough bed near the fire. Stones were already arranged there in a rectangle, and he piled springy heather between them. On the heather he spread moss from a basket at his side, and over the whole he threw a blanket.

"Would you like some porridge?" the woman asked Dummy. He was surprised to find that he could not bear the thought of eating—the very idea made him feel sick—so he shook his head.

"The friar has made the bed ready for you," the woman said. "I think you would be more comfortable there by the fire." She put out an arm to lift him to his feet and supported him as he tottered to the bed. He was glad that it was only a few steps, and glad, too, of her strong arm. She arranged some heather under his head as a pillow, covered him with another couple of blankets, and sat down again beside him.

"What's your name?" she asked.

He looked back at her without speaking. She exchanged glances with the friar across the open hearth.

"Whoever you are, you seem ill and you need to rest." Seeing his anxious look she went on. "You can sleep safely here."

Dummy did not feel at all sure that he was safe there, but it was such a relief to rest his body on the soft bed that he could not resist it. His head ached, he felt first hot and then cold, and every time he tried to sink into sleep he would begin to dream that he was being chased by Master and Roger—he could hear their footsteps crashing after him through the Forest. Exhausted as he was, he dozed fitfully, and heard other people entering and leaving the cave. At one moment he opened his eyes and saw a young man looking down at him.

"He hasn't spoken at all," said the woman. "And he's been badly beaten."

The young man turned away as he replied, and Dummy did not catch his first words, but then he heard ". . . could have sent him. How did he find us, anyway?"

Drifting in and out of consciousness Dummy heard the friar say ". . . a very small spy." Then he fell into a deep chasm of sleep. Much later he was woken from his nightmare by the friar saying, "Nobody's chasing you." He touched Dummy's burning face with a cool cloth.

IT WAS SEVERAL DAYS LATER when Dummy woke up feeling as if he had come to himself again. He was very weak, but the nightmares had vanished, and he felt alert, for the first time, to his strange surroundings. Where was he?

He knew that it must be daytime, because sunlight was filtering through the roof of the cave, casting pretty shadows on the walls. High up he could see ferns growing, and beneath them the long, tangly roots of a tree. The cave was big—nearly as big as Master's barn—with another cave opening out of it at one end. There were a number of beds like his own, all empty of occupants; in fact there was no one else in the cave, which made it easier to stare at everything. He tried stretching his body to see how it felt. It was still sore, but it felt much better. He raised himself cautiously on one elbow.

At that moment the woman came back into the cave and at once noticed he was awake. She came over to him, looking young and pretty with her cap of short black curls, and graceful in her tunic and leggings.

"Better?" she asked, and he nodded shyly. "I'm Marian, by the way, and that's Tucky over there. What's your name?" He looked awkwardly away. When he didn't answer she looked puzzled but then said, "Would you like some breakfast?"

There was something slightly rough and unsympathetic in her attitude to him. It was as if she was doing her human duty by him, and that was all. He nodded, and she returned with a plate of bread soaked in milk, which he ate slowly and with pleasure. It was sweet to the taste.

"Did you see your things?" she asked. She pointed at the neat pile she had made by Dummy's bed of his few possessions left after the headlong flight through the Forest. There was his scratching stick, which he had luckily kept tucked into his belt, a penny he had once found in the stable yard and hidden in the lining of his ragged breeches, and a small colored stone he had found in the brook and had kept, pretending it was a precious jewel.

"I washed your breeches," Marian explained, "and the friar has mended them."

She sat down on the earth floor beside him and looked searchingly at him. "What are you doing here?" she asked him, and then, when he didn't reply, added, "Who sent you?" Dummy slowly shook his head. "We have enemies," she went on, "who would give anything to find us and destroy us. Suppose what happened was that they got hold of you, and bribed you, or beat and frightened you, to follow us, find out about us, discover where we live, and then to go back to them and report? Is that what you are doing here?" She spoke more sternly to him now.

Appalled, Dummy shook his head again. If Marian believed he was a spy, perhaps she would have him killed.

"Very well, then," she said. "If you are not a spy, tell me how you come to be here. How did you find us?"

Hopelessly, Dummy put a finger on his lips and shook his head. He could feel the tears coming into his eyes and tried to fight them.

"You refuse to speak?"

Dummy held his tongue between finger and thumb and shook his head once more.

Marian looked at him in astonishment. "You are telling me that you *can't* speak? That you are dumb?"

Dummy nodded. Suddenly, Marian got up and left the underground cave, and Dummy lay in his bed, thinking miserably that he had offended her. In a few minutes, however, she was back with a young man.

He was handsome, slim, of medium height. He had red hair and the most brilliant blue eyes Dummy had ever seen. He came and sat down beside Dummy's bed and regarded him thoughtfully.

"You cannot speak?" he asked him. Dummy nodded.

"So we cannot ask you any questions," the man said. "It is convenient for you, is it not?"

Dummy looked at him in puzzlement.

"You are very small to be a spy, if that is what you are. But let me tell you something. I am responsible for the safety of many men, and if you do anything to bring them into danger I should have to kill you, young as you are, because you would be doing a man's work. As it is, you will have to stay here with us—we cannot let you go—so that you will be, in a sense, our prisoner. If you attempt to run away . . ."

Dummy shook his head, his dark eyes fixed on the man's bright blue eyes.

"With respect, Robin," put in Tucky from the other side of the room, "he could just be an apprentice who was starved and beaten and who ran away. That's not so unusual."

"And how would he find his way here? It's so

well hidden that sometimes I can barely find the entrance myself."

"The hand of God," said Tucky, but Dummy could see the others were unconvinced. There *was* something mysterious in the way he had tumbled into the outlaws' hideaway. It puzzled him too.

Meanwhile he had something else important to think about. Tucky's casual use of the young man's name had brought back many overheard conversations in the village. The great Forest, Dummy had heard, was the home of dangerous outlaws who would rob you and kill you as soon as look at you, and the best-known outlaw of all was Robin Hood. Master had particularly feared and detested Robin Hood, because he was said to take from rich people and give to poor people, and Master hated poor people. Robin Hood had a woman friend called Marian, and was attended by a friar called Tuck, so all the evidence was there. Could he possibly have fallen into the clutches of Robin Hood and his Men?

It seemed a desperate situation in which to find himself, and yet, despite Robin's threat, no one had actually hurt him. So far it seemed better than living with Master—at least there was more to eat. But Robin had made it quite clear that they were still wondering whether he was a spy. He had no idea how he could convince them otherwise.

Later that day, ignored by everyone, Dummy struggled out of his heather bed, taking his scratching stick with him, and began to walk shakily about the cave. He noticed the hole in the wall through which he had shot into this new world. Then he discovered a flight of earthen steps, and slowly, on legs that wobbled, he climbed up and out into the sunlight. He found himself standing close to a huge oak tree with widespreading mossy roots, full of little crevices. The tree stood on a small, rocky mound with a wide green sward to one side of it, and a meadow beyond. At first Dummy looked about him nervously, as if he might find Master and Roger waiting outside, but then he saw the dense thicket of thorn and briar and bramble that surrounded the area, and he realized that these people were well protected, that the thicket bounded a tiny kingdom.

Exhausted by his small effort, Dummy sat for a few moments among the oak tree roots, getting his breath back. It was good to feel the warmth of the sun on his legs and to see a bright drift of bluebells between him and the thicket. He heard the song of the cuckoo. But he could not feel confident he was out of trouble. He had escaped from Master but had fallen in with a dangerous parcel of gangsters who might decide to kill him at any time. He must be endlessly watchful for danger.

Needing his old comfort, he took his stick and scratched his secret sign among the fallen acorns at the foot of the tree. It was satisfying to see it there, but when he had finished he rubbed it out with his foot and hid the stick with care in a small crevice in the oak tree. A huge black dog came and sat beside him, resting its head upon Dummy's thigh. Later Marian called to it. "Midnight! Here, boy!"

After Dummy had sat there for a bit, a man came up from down below and introduced himself as Will Stutely. He carried a bundle of goose quills, and from a bag he took some straight sticks of birch. With a sharp knife he cut the quills and began to insert three feathered pieces into the hafts of the sticks. Dummy realized they were arrows. As Will finished each one, he trimmed the feathers to make them even.

After a while, he handed Dummy a knife and a quill and demonstrated how to cut each one into four. Dummy was clumsy at first, cutting them unevenly and spoiling several quills, but finally he feathered an arrow that looked a little bit like Will's.

"Well done, lad," said Will. Dummy continued to watch him at work. Will was dressed in green, as Marian was. He wore a green tunic and hose, a leather belt around his waist, and a green hood on his shoulders.

Presently two more men in green entered the clearing, carrying a dead deer slung from a branch between them. They laid it down on the turf and began the long task of skinning it and preparing it for food.

Despite his fears Dummy felt good. The sun warmed him, Will had praised him, and he felt there were worse fates than to be out in this beautiful Forest full of the spring song of birds. Perhaps he was safe after all.

FOUR

Making Friends

By THE END of that first waking day Dummy had
learned that the big oak tree under which he and
Will had sat was called the Trystell Tree, meaning
the place where all of them met together. It was a
tree of enormous width with huge branches into
which it was easy to climb.

Dummy could not work out how many Men
Robin had at his command. As the evening wore
on, more and more Men appeared, all of them wearing the same costume of dull green. Dummy saw
how well it blended with the deep greens of the Forest; among the trees the Men quickly became almost invisible. They came out of its shadowy
depths, some returning from hunting, others coming with bags of money, which they deposited in
front of Robin at the foot of the Trystell Tree.
Three or four looked as if they had been in a fight
and recounted their adventures to much laughter.

The next day Dummy began to explore a bit farther, and he found that if he took another path through the crags he came upon a Ravine where the land split open. The Men used the floor of the Ravine, he discovered, for archery and quarterstaff fighting, for swordplay and wrestling. They called the place the Field of Practice.

Back at the Tree itself Tucky had a huge outdoor kitchen—a fireplace protected from drafts by a careful arrangement of hedges, with a chimney made of bricks. It had a spit upon its hearth. In the cave beneath, as Dummy knew, were shelves with Tucky's enormous collection of spices, dried herbs and mushrooms, peas and beans and meal. On the second morning, Tucky, who seemed, unlike Marian and Robin, to have no fears or suspicions of Dummy, gave him a generous slice of maslin bread spread with goose grease, and he ate it with pleasure.

Tucky showed him the Meadow, where the outlaws kept their horses. They had five. In the winter the horses were stabled in one of the caves.

"I can see you like horses," Tucky said, as Dummy fearlessly went up to them and rubbed their noses.

They were standing beneath a tall oak tree when there was a violent rustling in the branches overhead, and a boy fell to the ground with a hard thump. He lay there for a moment as if stunned, then rose to his feet, gave a broad grin at Tucky and Dummy, and limped away.

"That's Jehan!" said Tucky. "He's a handful, that one, always in trouble!" But Tucky sounded as if he liked Jehan, and Dummy could see why. He was a good-looking boy with carroty-colored hair and freckles, and there was something merry about him, even as he picked himself up from his fall. Dummy thought he'd like to have a boy like that as his friend.

Then Tucky showed him what he called the Oratory of Our Lady of the Forest, a grassy clearing where the branches interlaced overhead, giving a soft green light. Between the branches there was a long view to distant blue hills. There was a fallen treetrunk covered in moss, and Tucky sat down upon it.

"Robin and I both like to come here," the friar said. "Robin says that we are under the protection of Our Lady of the Forest. We need to be," he continued after a pause. "Robin has enemies who hate him and who seek to destroy him." Suddenly he looked sharply at Dummy. "I hope you are not one of them." Dummy shook his head vehemently, and after a long look Tucky said, "You look a nice boy to me. But what do I know of the world?"

WITHIN A FEW DAYS Dummy began to grow stronger. Tucky gave him a sweet, delicious linctus that seemed to ease his troublesome cough, and the regular meals made him feel healthy and happy. He could still sense Marian regarding him with suspicion, and a certain coolness in Robin, but the rest of the Men tended to spoil him.

Will Stutely, who had felt like a friend since that first day when he had shown him how to cut the quills, had carved him a little set of panpipes out of a piece of boxwood. Sitting outside in the sun in the roots of the oak tree, Dummy had watched the broad fingers working with surprising delicacy, and when Will had finished, and polished his work with methodical patience, he had suddenly turned and handed the pipes to him.

"They're for you," he said.

Dummy put out a trembling hand and took the flute, feeling the wood satin-smooth beneath his fingers. Shyly, because Will was watching, he blew, and a strange, strangled note came out. He blew again, harder, and the note was harsh and shrill. The next note sounded right, and he added another and another, in a simple tune. Suddenly, to his shame he felt himself crying, because it seemed the pipes were speaking for him.

For many days after that Dummy practiced on the pipes snatches of tunes he had heard, and imitations of birdcalls. There was a song about life in the Forest that the Men sometimes sang, and after many attempts he managed to play its intricate tune. He was delighted with himself.

There were other discoveries too. One of the youngest of the Men, Thomas Tyndal, not much more than a boy, brought him his collection of birds' eggs and showed each one to him, tossing his thick fair hair out of his eyes.

"See, this little one is a robin's, and the speckledy one is a blackbird's. The blue one with the black spots is a song thrush's. The creamy white one is a woodpecker's."

Dummy picked up the lovely delicate things one by one, admiring the color and the tiny markings.

"They are for you," said Thomas. "I'd like you to have them." Dummy could not believe his generosity.

But more than ever Dummy wanted carroty-haired Jehan as his friend. Despite his earlier tumble Jehan seemed fearless, swinging from branch to branch in the treetops in a way that made Dummy's heart contract. He even hung upside down from the Trystell Tree, his feet locked in the branches, his mop of orange curls swinging. He seemed a clever boy too. One day Dummy saw him scratching signs on a tablet with a stylus and knew that that was what he had once done, back in the good days before he had known Master, and what he had tried again to do in the stable.

"Can you write?" Jehan asked him, as he saw Dummy watching him closely. Dummy shook his head. He minded very much not being able to talk to Jehan and thought how boring that must make him seem. But he had learned something new: "writing" was the word for scratching signs.

One day, when he was sitting among the tree

roots picking out a tune on the pipes, Jehan came and sat down beside him.

"Could you show me how to do that?" he asked in his friendly way, and note by note Dummy taught him the tune.

On another day Jehan was grooming the horses in the Meadow, and Dummy stopped to give him a hand. They worked side by side, sweating a little under the midday sun, and then Jehan said, "Can you ride?" Dummy nodded. He knew he could ride, had known how ever since he could remember. Together, they saddled two of the horses—a lively young chestnut for Jehan and a slower old fellow for Dummy. With a leg up from Jehan, Dummy swung into the saddle and at once felt a kind of joy and energy he remembered from long ago. They moved along the Meadow and out into the Forest, gradually picking up speed.

"You *can* ride!" Jehan said in honest admiration, as Dummy persuaded the old horse into a willing gallop. "You need a better horse than old Harry. I shall ask Robin if you can ride Star. Only our best horsemen ride him."

ONE AFTERNOON, when Dummy was helping Tucky with the vegetables for the soup, chopping turnips with a big knife, Tucky began to tell him a bit about some of the Men.

"Much over there," he said, indicating the little tailor who sat cross-legged, sewing green suits for the Men, "he used to be a miller until Prince John had him turned out of his mill. And your friend Jehan's father, Gilbert of the White Hand, had his property stolen by the Prince to add to his own lands, because he refused to give up a horse Prince John wanted."

Seeing the question in Dummy's eyes, Tucky went on, "You know, of course, that our rightful king is King Richard. But he went to the Crusades—years ago now—and nobody knows what became of him. Some say he is killed; others, that he is imprisoned. Anyway, his brother, Prince John, behaves as if he is already crowned king. And Prince John"—here Tucky pounded a piece of meat as angrily as if he were pounding Prince John himself—"is not a good prince. Or a good man. Nearly all the outlaws live out here in the Forest because they are in danger from the Prince."

Suddenly there was a big voice shouting outside, and a loud bark from Midnight, and Dummy started with terror in a way he had not done recently.

"It's all right," Tucky said quickly. "Come and say hello. Unless I'm mistaken, Little John's come back to us."

There was no one under the Trystell Tree, however, but a huge fellow, head and shoulders bigger than any of the other outlaws. From the greeting he received, Dummy slowly realized that his name must be a joke. Little John noticed everyone and spoke to each in turn, even giving Dummy a long, thoughtful glance.

"So that's your spy, Robin," Dummy heard him say afterward in a booming voice. "You must be losing your nerve if you're afraid of that little chap."

"Marian thinks he might have been sent here to report on our movements to the Sheriff."

"Marian worries too much about you. Have sense. He's just a poor kid who's run away."

"But how did he find us? It does seem odd."

"You're a believing man. The angels may have sent him. And you'd better show them that you appreciate the gift."

Dummy felt full of gratitude to Little John for his words. Gradually, he thought, the Men would come to believe he wanted to be their friend. Although Marian still treated Dummy with suspicion, with Robin he was becoming a favorite. Robin had given him a name, Bird, because he said that he dropped into the Hideaway like a young bird falling out of its nest.

Robin often woke Dummy and took him on early morning trips into the Forest. At sunrise, Dummy discovered, the whole animal world was out and about enjoying the morning—the vixen with her cubs, the birds finding food for their nestlings. On the first morning he went out with Robin they saw a doe, her beautiful flanks spotted, raising her head and listening alertly, her tiny baby behind her. Then suddenly the Forest came alive, as the rest of the herd, hitherto invisible in the trees, got wind of Robin and Dummy. The deer sprang away with such grace and speed that Dummy felt his eyes prick with tears at the beauty of it. How could Robin love the deer so much, he wondered, yet kill them for food? Though he longed to ask, he could not. He mouthed sounds to himself, but no words came. Only when he played his pipes did he feel as if he had a voice. As the music played and others listened, it felt as if for once he was having a conversation.

On another day Robin led him past a pile of rocks and down a long track through the brilliant green of the young bracken.

"Close your eyes, Bird!" he commanded, and he guided him for another few minutes. "Now open them."

Dummy opened his eyes upon a wide, clear pool that reflected the blue sky. Around it, their slender branches bending toward the water, were trees covered in a lace of white blossom.

"We call this the Secret Lake," Robin said. "No one ever comes here but us."

Sometimes Robin took Dummy with him beyond the Forest, and Dummy quickly discovered that Robin had many friends outside it, among both rich and poor. One cold April day Robin borrowed a horse and cart from a farmer in Mansfield and loaded it with sticks and peat, with milk and eggs and bread and ale. They went first to a poor family in Southwell, where several small children were huddled with their mother around a tiny fire. Dummy built up the fire, while Robin unpacked the food, and also, Dummy could not help noticing, hid a silver piece beneath the bobbin on the spinning wheel. The man of the house, he knew, had been thrown into prison by the Sheriff of Nottingham. In another cottage, where an old couple was sick in bed, Robin swept the hearth, built a fire, and made them some soup; and in a third he nursed a sick baby, told the children a story, and assured the wife that he would save her husband from the gallows. Dummy loved to see the sad, pale faces regaining hope as Robin found ways to cheer and comfort the families. It puzzled him that people like Master feared Robin so much, when he was always so kind.

FIVE

Robin to the Rescue

THE NEXT DAY was one Dummy never forgot. He was in a deep sleep when he heard Robin whisper, "Come with me, Bird. We have work to do." He longed to go on sleeping, but he knew he must obey Robin's command, and in a few moments he was out of his warm bed, pulling on his breeches, and splashing cold water on his face.

When he joined Robin outside, Dummy scarcely recognized him. Robin was not wearing his short tunic of Lincoln green over dark green hose, with shoes and hood of green-dyed leather. Instead he wore the long serge robe of a monk, a patched white garment with a cowl. He had sandals upon his bare feet. Dummy could not conceal his surprise.

"A shock, eh, Bird?" laughed Robin. "This is a day for a good disguise."

The two of them set off on the long walk to Nottingham, though a kindly farmer took them part of the way in his cart. It was midday before they reached the city, and they were both thirsty. As they turned in at an alehouse, Robin, Dummy noticed, no longer walked with the long stride of the hunter but with the slow, short step of man accustomed to pace a cloister, reading as he walked. They sat on a bench by a filthy, stained table. With the timid gesture of one unused to the world, Robin called to the landlord in a high, reedy voice.

The landlord tried to ignore him at first. "I don't want no monks begging in here, Joan," he muttered to his wife. "Let me have customers who can pay for their drink."

"I have money," Robin answered. He took out a coin and laid it on the table in front of him. Joan came to serve him.

"Don't you pay no attention to him, Father," she said. "Me, I'm glad enough to have a holy gentleman like yourself in here—it's a privilege. What brings you out of the cloister to this godforsaken place?"

"No place is without God's love," said Robin piously. "I am come to Nottingham to fetch this lad, a novice who is joining the Abbey of Rievaulx."

"You are come a long way, Father, for such a scrap of a lad."

"We need to quench our thirst before we travel on," said Robin, "and to find out what local news there is to take back to my brethren at Rievaulx."

"News?" said Joan, wiping the perspiration off her face with the end of her long sleeve and turning to her husband. "Have we any news, Master Gregory?"

The landlord thought for a moment. "There's a hanging this afternoon," he said. "Laborer Tom caught red-handed shooting a deer. I might go along to watch that."

"I'm glad to hear it," said Robin righteously. "Venison is not fit meat for peasants, and all should know it."

"I did hear that he's got small children at home and nothing to feed them on," said Joan, pity in her voice.

"Stealing is a grave sin," said Robin, shaking his head. "And doubly wrong when it is thieving the king's property."

"But when people are hungry," Joan said doubtfully, "and all those great fat deer wander about in the Forest . . ."

"Landlord," said Robin sharply. "Your wife's tongue is running away with her. She will be talking treason next."

"Be quiet, Mistress," said the landlord, looking anxious.

"Any more news?" asked Robin.

"There's the shooting match at Corpus Christi," said the landlord, more respectful of his customer since the mention of treason. "Sheriff organized it. Men are coming from all over to take part. But that wouldn't interest a man like yourself."

"It would interest my brothers back in the cloister," Robin said. "They love to hear how the world goes. What is the prize?"

"An arrow of the purest beaten gold," said the landlord. "Our Sheriff does things handsomely when he's a mind."

"He wastes our taxes," Joan grumbled to herself, but her husband, who clearly liked the thought of the contest, paid no attention to her.

They left the alehouse and Robin walked on, with a slow, stumbling gait that Dummy found hard to match, to the Sheriff of Nottingham's house, pausing only at a butcher's shop in the public square where Robin conferred with the shopkeeper. Dummy watched fascinated as a big wooden scaffold, a platform with a gibbet on the top, was erected in the middle of the square. On the far side of the scaffold stood the magnificent house that belonged to the Sheriff. It was so big that it took up one whole side of the square, its black and white timbers hanging over the street. By chance the Sheriff himself stood on the doorstep, talking to a departing guest. He wore a fine crimson robe, trimmed with fur, over his full belly. His broad crimson hat matched the color of his cheeks.

Robin stood beside the steps, head meekly bowed beneath his cowl, arms tucked in his long sleeves.

"Sir," he began, in a high, timid voice. The Sheriff, who was calling a witticism after his guests, ignored him.

"Sir!" Robin said again, as the Sheriff turned. The Sheriff paused for a moment, one foot on the threshold, and looked at him.

"I am offering myself as confessor," Robin said. "For the man who is to be hanged this afternoon."

"Do you know him?" the Sheriff asked crossly.

"I am passing through this town, and heard of his fate. It seemed to me that God has called me to minister to this poor man."

"He richly deserves to die."

"Of course. But a pious, God-fearing man such as yourself would not wish to refuse him absolution before he dies. And I shall instruct him to pray for you in his last prayers."

Dummy knew, because Robin had told him, that only the year before a man who was hanged had publicly cursed the Sheriff with his dying breath, and the very next day the Sheriff's favorite horse had sickened and died. The story of this, and also of the Sheriff's superstitious fear, had been all over town.

"Very well," said the Sheriff. "It can do no harm."

"And shall I get paid for my service?" asked Robin.

"I thought God had called you to perform it," said the Sheriff sharply. "Is not that payment enough?"

"A poor monk must live, sir," Robin replied meekly.

"Must drink, you probably mean," said the

Sheriff contemptuously, but he pulled a silver coin out of his pocket and threw it at Robin so that it fell on the pavement and Robin had to scramble for it in the gutter. The Sheriff laughed, went into his house, and shut the door.

"Do you know the way from here to the blasted oak?" Robin suddenly asked Dummy. "The hollow oak by the track we passed as we came out of the Forest this morning?"

Dummy had a good sense of direction and he nodded eagerly.

"Leave me for a while," said Robin. "But stay near me in the crowd this afternoon and watch what happens. When it's all over I will meet you by the oak." He gave Dummy money to buy bread and cheese, turned on his heel, and disappeared in the direction of the town jail.

That afternoon Dummy watched as Robin walked with the criminal, Tom, through the streets of Nottingham. When men were executed they were first heavily beaten at the jail, then tied to a shutter and dragged through the streets at the tail of a cart. On the scaffold itself they were strung up to be hanged, then, before they were quite dead, they were cut down and disemboweled. It was a terrible death.

As the procession wound through the streets from the jail, citizens lined the route, fascinated at the sight of the pale criminal, already covered in blood, his eyes rolling in his head with terror, his head bumping along in the dirt and dust of the road.

Dummy heard him muttering prayers to Mary and to Jesus, occasionally calling out the names of his wife and children.

Robin paced slowly behind him, intoning pious sentences out loud. "Think upon your sins, which are many. Let this be a sign to all who are tempted to wrongdoing. We shall see justice done this day."

Once or twice he bent down and lifted Tom's head, holding it out of the mire, and he seemed to be conferring with him. Dummy wondered what he could be saying. When they reached the public square the drums began to beat more insistently, and the executioner waited on the platform beneath the gibbet with several assistants beside him. At the Sheriff's house one of the casements of an upstairs window had been removed, and the Sheriff and his wife stood at the window waiting to see justice done. Tom staggered so much when they untied him from the shutter that he could scarcely walk, and Robin was obliged to help him to his feet, which he did coldly and unsympathetically. The executioner bade them mount the scaffold, but Robin demurred.

"I must hear this man's confession in a private place," he announced. "I must grant him absolution and give him time to say prayers of penance, including a prayer for Sir Sheriff. If the butcher will grant us the use of his shop for a few minutes, this will be quickly accomplished."

The executioner looked up at the Sheriff for permission. The square was full of people who would be shocked if the monk's plea was refused. The Sheriff nodded at the executioner, and the monk helped the half-fainting man into the butcher's shop and shut the door.

As the sun shone brightly down on the public square, the crowd speculated about what sins Tom was confessing.

"Please, Father, I stole a kiss from Betsy Watkins," one onlooker shouted out.

"Oh, my son, that is very wicked, even worse than stealing a deer," cried another.

"I nicked a purse from the Sheriff's servant."

"A thousand Hail Marys for you!"

Dummy could see that the Sheriff suspected he was being mocked and that he did not like being kept waiting for the execution any more than the crowd did.

"Go and knock on the door," he called to the executioner. "Tell them to hurry up."

The executioner did as he was told, and the crowd waited for another few minutes. Finally, at a nod from the Sheriff, the executioner tried to open the door, only to find that it was locked from within. He banged and rattled at it, but it did not open. Finally, using his strong shoulder, he forced the lock and disappeared inside. Almost at once he reappeared with the monk's white robe in his arms and a look of horror on his face.

"They are gone, Sir Sheriff," he stammered. "The shop is empty, and the gate into the lane at the back hangs open."

The Sheriff stared down at him unbelievingly.

"There was something else too. Written in blood from the butcher's offal pail there were some words scribbled on the wall."

"What words?" asked the Sheriff.

" 'Robin Hood,' my lord."

It took a moment for the Sheriff to recover from his surprise, but then he began shouting orders, orders that could barely be heard over the noise of the crowd. For its mood had changed, Dummy saw. A few minutes before, the crowd had thought only of seeing Tom killed. Now, thanks to Robin's bravery and audacity, they wanted Tom to escape. They laughed scornfully at the expression of outrage on the Sheriff's purple face. Clusters of mocking people gathered at the roads leading out of the square. They jeered at the Sheriff's sergeants, who were trying to set out in search of Tom and Robin. More important, they kept them from leaving. Much time elapsed before the Sheriff's horsemen managed to ride away.

With some difficulty Dummy struggled through the crowds and made his way to the oak tree by the track. At first he could see no sign of Robin, but suddenly there was a merry shout, and Robin swung down from the branches. A moment later Tom's scared face appeared among the leaves.

"That was a good day, Bird," Robin said triumphantly. Dummy noticed that he seemed exhilarated, and had a feeling that danger always made Robin excited. Later, as he picked out a new tune on his pipes, Dummy listened to poor Tom stammering out his gratitude.

"If it wasn't for you I would have been dead these last six hours," he said to Robin. "How can I thank you?"

"One day," said Robin, "we may need our friends to rise up in our defense, but in the meantime go to your wife and family, now safely far away in Yorkshire, and live in gratitude to God for sparing you." Tom nodded.

Dummy realized that his old master had simply been wrong about Robin Hood, as he had been wrong about many things. Robin was a hero, and, one day, he hoped, he would be just like him.

SIX

Dummy
the Bowman

BY THE TIME Dummy had spent several weeks in the Forest, he had grown fatter and much stronger. He had learned a lot, too, from living with the Men.

One morning Robin sat, as he often did, in his big carved chair by the Trystell Tree, listening and talking. Sometimes he talked to a man alone, and sometimes to three or four at a time. Watching and listening at a distance, Dummy heard snatches of conversation—"evicted from their cottage," "forced to sell their cattle," "imprisoned by the Sheriff," "likely to be hanged," "gone into hiding," "too poor to have a funeral"—as Robin gravely questioned the Men bringing back reports of what they had discovered. Dummy also listened to stories that made everyone shout with laughter—of skirmishes with the Sheriff of Nottingham's men, of assuming disguises to fool them and to help people escape, of taking money from greedy abbots who lived like princes and giving it to those who could not afford the simple necessities of life. Robin paid close attention as his Men gave their descriptions or their ideas about what should be done, and often asked others to comment and say what they thought. Then he spoke swiftly, with the clarity of a born leader.

After several hours, Robin broke off, beckoned to Dummy, and invited him to accompany him. Then he whistled to Midnight, who bounded up to go with them.

First they went to Our Lady of the Forest, Robin genuflecting as he entered as if he was in a real church, and then he knelt facing toward the blue hills. Dummy sat a little shyly on the fallen tree-trunk. He knew that Robin was praying and wondered if he was remembering the peasants cruelly taxed by greedy lords, the poor people starving and wretched under a harsh prince yet punished if they killed a deer or even a hare to feed their children. It was very peaceful sitting there in the Oratory, and Dummy sank into a kind of reverie that was broken by Robin.

"Because you are a good companion to me, Bird, I have decided to trust you, young as you are, and to treat you as a citizen of Robin's Country. We shall teach you to shoot and to fight with a stave. In fact, I will choose a piece of yew and start to make you a bow this very day."

Dummy admired Robin so much, and longed so badly to feel accepted by him, that he was delighted by these words. They walked together for some distance among the great oaks, and the slender birches with their pale trunks and trembling leaves, the sun casting dappled shadows on the ground between the branches. Eventually they came to a fine yew, a dark, graceful presence in its clearing.

"The very best bows," Robin explained, "come from the trunk of the tree, but those are for practiced bowmen. We all learn to shoot, however, with a boughstave bow, a bow cut from one of the branches. It need not be from yew—elm or ash are very good—but here in Sherwood we have a number of fine yews, and this is the wood we prefer."

Robin examined the branches with care, holding them in his hand as if weighing them, and finally took out his knife and cut the gently curving bough carefully from the tree. Dummy carried it back to Robin's Country full of pride.

"By the way," Robin told him, "Marian will teach you to shoot."

Dummy's face fell. He felt Marian did not like him, and it seemed odd, living among so many men, to be taught archery by a woman.

"She is the best archer among us," Robin went on, as if answering his thought.

Then Robin returned to his grave discussions at the Trystell Tree while Will Stutely undertook to help Bird make his bow.

"The bough is too thick," said Will, "so we will split it down the grain." This he carefully did, setting half aside to make another bow. He had Dummy remove the bark and then sent him off to

Tucky for a jar of the oil made from flax seed. Meanwhile he started shaping the bow by cutting away the surplus wood with an ax, and as the graceful form gradually emerged he began bending it. Again and again he asked Dummy to rub the bow with the oil to make it supple, while he worked on it again with a drawknife.

"Owning a bow for the first time is a very important moment," said Will. "It really makes you one of us. A good bow is like a friend," he went on. "It will go everywhere with you, keep you company, and protect you in danger. A youngster like you needs a bow that is suitable for his own strength. When you get older you will need a stronger one, but this will be with you for many a month yet."

Will attached a string to test what he called "the fistmele," the distance between the string and the bow. For this he made Dummy spread out his small hand and used the distance between his thumb and the spread of his fingers. Then he returned to the delicate task of finishing the bow with a spokeshave. He had Dummy scrape the bow gently with a knife, then rub it hard with the wood shavings to give it a smooth satin finish.

It was a long, slow process, and Dummy, wiping the sweat out of his eyes, got very tired. Sometimes Will took a turn at rubbing the bow while Dummy rested.

"You're a hard little worker," Will said, and Dummy felt full of pride.

The sun was going down by the time the bow was finished to Will's satisfaction, and then he helped Dummy make a handle with a strip of leather glued into place.

Just as it began to grow dark, Will cut the nocks in the ends of the bow that would hold the linen string, and when Dummy had dressed the ends with beeswax, Will strung the bow and it was ready for use. Since special arrows would be needed to fit Dummy's small bow, he could not, to his disappointment, begin to shoot at once, but Will promised to make him some arrows first thing in the morning.

When he went to bed that night Dummy laid his bow down beside him, as all the other outlaws did, and when he dreamed, he dreamed of shooting it.

As he found next morning, the reality was much harder.

"Come," said Marian coldly after breakfast. "We will go into the Forest." She walked silently ahead of him.

"This is as good a place as any," she said when they came to a clearing. Then she showed him how to stand with his feet pointing sideways, a shoulder's width apart, in the stance he had already noted in the Men, neither stooping nor quite upright.

With an empty bow he practiced drawing the bow back to his ear, his left hand a little above his right.

"Now, try nocking an arrow to the string," said Marian. "When you shoot it you only use your three middle fingers, never your thumb or your little finger—we call them the two demons because archers say they bring bad luck. Don't cock your wrist or the arrow will fall off the rest. Close your left eye."

It felt very strange, bending the stiff bow, and trying to keep the arrow in place.

"Pull back so that about four fingers of arrow stick out beyond the bow. Hold it. Now loose the arrow." Somehow Dummy muffed loosing it, and it fell at his feet. So did the next arrow. And the next.

"You haven't been listening to me," Marian said, rather sharply, he thought. When he failed again she said cuttingly, "Perhaps you don't have the gift. Some people don't." What Dummy wanted to say, but could not, was that if she was not so cross with him, he might be able to do it. He tried again, and the arrow once more failed to shoot. He threw down the bow and turned away, angry and humiliated. He picked up a stone and threw it furiously, blindly, at a tree. There was a long silence.

"Right," said Marian. "Try again!"

Slowly, sulkily, because he hated her by now but did not quite dare to disobey, Dummy turned back and picked up the bow and fitted another arrow to the string. This time he did not try as hard as he had tried before, he was so sure that he could not do it. He pulled back the string strongly, closed his left eye, let go with his right hand, and his arrow sang twenty feet through the air and hit a treetrunk with a satisfying *thunk*.

"That's more like it," said Marian. "Archers talk

about shooting from their hearts. That arrow came from deep inside you."

She stayed silent all the way back to Robin's Country, but just before they got there she remarked, "Robin has asked me to give you a lesson every day. I shall expect you to practice by yourself. Practice is what makes an archer. It gets very boring, but you have to persist. Becoming a great archer is not about being a brilliant hunter or being able to kill an enemy a bowshot away. It's about victory over oneself."

Dummy was not really sure what she meant and hoped she would say more, but she fell back into silence. He *did* mean to practice, though, if only to show her that he was not as hopeless as she thought.

The next day his shooting was better, perhaps because he had got up very early and spent an hour in the Forest trying to hit a target stuck on an old oak tree.

"It's not enough to hit the target," Marian said later. "What matters is shooting the arrow as well as you can. Naturally, if you do prepare properly and shoot the arrow perfectly you will hit the target, but at the moment all you have to worry about is doing it correctly. Plant your feet, draw the bow, close your eye, loose the arrow. . . . Mmm . . . better. Not very good, but better."

One day, Dummy swore to himself, he would force her to say that he had shot well.

Summer

SEVEN

The Long Day

EVERY DAY Marian gave Dummy a shooting lesson, and every day he continued to practice alone in the Forest. He felt too shy of his skills to join the Men in their practice, although he enjoyed watching them and trying to learn from them.

Hard as he worked, however, Marian still did not seem satisfied.

One day she said, "You try too hard to impress me. Or to impress yourself, wanting to be clever at shooting. You want to be better than other people, to be admired—it gets in the way. Forget that. Do it for its own sake. And because you love it."

This stung Dummy. He left her, his cheeks red with anger, and went straight to ride Star. As he galloped down one of the Forest rides, he suddenly, unwillingly, recognized the truth of what Marian had just said. He rode well because he loved to ride and not because he wanted admiration or to be better than others. He *liked* being admired and told he did it well, of course he did, but it was unimportant compared to the pleasure of feeling a horse moving under him and the wind in his hair. Perhaps one day he would feel the same way about shooting.

THERE WAS MUCH going on in Robin's Country now that high summer had come. The Men were practicing for the shooting contest at the Long Day Feast; Tucky was working hard to prepare for the Feast itself and was grateful for Dummy's help.

The friar was baking pies, which he placed in his cool underground larder. Marian, who usually avoided domestic tasks, helped him, gutting chickens and cleaning rabbits with speed and skill. She showed Dummy how to pluck a chicken without breaking the skin and how to put a hand inside its little body and pull out the guts neatly and swiftly in a single action.

Some of the Men came back with bushels of strawberries given by the people of a village who had reason to love Robin Hood. Dummy helped pound them into a delicious mess, to be eaten with thick yellow cream. He couldn't help eating some of it himself, but no one chided or beat him for it, as Master or Mistress would have done.

"That's right!" Tucky would say. "Eat all you can. You're still but half a boy yet, and who needs our food more than you?"

The day of the Feast itself was clear and sunny. Early in the morning they dragged out tables from the Hideaway and set them in a horseshoe in the long, grassy slope called the Pleasaunce. Then they covered them with the tablecloths that had previously been set upon the thornbushes to bleach. The cloths were decorated with sprays of sweet-smelling honeysuckle and fresh green leaves, and were set with knives for eating and goblets for drinking.

Dummy cleaned and trimmed all the lanterns that would stand on a pathway between the Trystell Tree and the Pleasaunce. They were made of horn, and the light of the candles would shine out prettily in the dark. On the tables there stood rushlights, tiny saucers holding a wick made out of rush that soaked up oil.

After that his task was to chop carrots and turnips for broth and to grind meal in the quern until his arms ached. Meanwhile Marian was cutting the trenchers of bread that served as plates for each person who dined, and Tom Tyndal was plucking the swan for the second course of the dinner.

Dummy felt excited about the Feast. Friends and helpers of Robin from all the towns and villages round about would come to join the Men, and they would feast and drink far into the night.

There was another reason for his excitement. Several days before, when Marian was giving him his shooting lesson as usual, she had said to him, "You must enter for the shooting competition on the Long Day." Seeing the surprise on his face she went on. "It will be good practice for you." She paused and then added, "You have worked hard.

One day you will be a fine bowman." It was the first praise he had had from her, and he could not help smiling with pleasure. "You've got a long way to go yet, mind you," she added. He nodded. But Marian's few words of kindness would make it a great deal easier to continue.

On the afternoon of the Feast, Little John called for the archers to take their place before the targets, starting with the youngest first. They were given a mark much nearer to the target than their experienced elders.

"Come, Tom!" Little John said. "Show us your skills, for I know you have practiced hard all spring."

"One moment," said Marian. "If the youngest must shoot first, then we have a younger candidate than Tom. Bird here must try his skill."

Obviously surprised, Little John agreed. At this early stage of the competition there were few spectators. Many of the Men were still helping with the preparations for the Feast; others were waiting until the older archers had their turn. All the same, Dummy could feel his legs trembling at the idea of standing up before them all, but he tried to remember Marian's lessons about doing things for their own sake. Not for himself.

He removed an arrow from the quiver as slowly as he dared, wishing he might never have to shoot it. Suppose it flew only a few yards! He tried to stand straight and steady at the mark as Marian had taught him, to breathe deeply and relax, to pull back the string steadily and loose the arrow smoothly. To his delight the arrow flew straight and strong, singing toward the target where it embedded itself in one of the outer circles.

Little John and Tom were speechless, as if unable to believe their eyes. Then they and the Men sitting around the butts applauded.

Now Dummy felt much more confident. He had been well taught, and he knew just what to do. He nocked another arrow, followed the practice Marian had taught him, and once again he hit the target, this time nearer to the center. Jehan, lying on the ground as he watched, gave a cheer and a shout.

As he reached for his last arrow Dummy saw that more of the Men were beginning to arrive at the butts, attracted by the clapping and Jehan's shout. He felt rather pleased—now he *wanted* people to see how well he could shoot. Then he noticed Robin among them, trying to stand back and not be seen, probably for fear of distracting Dummy. With an effort Dummy pushed every thought out of his mind except shooting.

"Don't try too hard to hit the target," he heard Marian's voice in his head. "That will make you tense. Concentrate on shooting as well as you can. Point your arrow toward the target as if you loved it."

He took two more deep breaths, then held up his bow. He felt as if it was a part of himself, that when he drew its long supple length, pulling back the rough string, it was an extension of his body.

The arrow left him without a jerk and flew gracefully through the air. And yes, he had got it into the inner ring of the target.

This time all the Men shouted together and threw their caps into the air, and Robin came across the grass to Dummy, smiling at his triumph.

"Your teacher must be proud of you," said Robin. Secretly Dummy doubted this. "You shall have a prize of a silver sixpence."

Marian nodded at Dummy, the only praise she gave him, but the Men came up to him one at a time, congratulating him on his skill.

The Men continued to compete, shooting over longer and longer distances, and eventually only Marian and Robin were left in the contest. Marian shot first, a marvelous shot, in the inner ring of the bull's-eye. Robin's shot followed, nicking her gray goose feather.

"Enough!" said Robin. "We are equal in skill; we will share the prize together." The prize was a huge flask of southern wine.

Dummy recalled his duties as junior cook and made his way back to Tucky with a swagger in his step. The friar looked up from the spit where he was roasting venison and smiled amiably at him.

"I suppose you're too high and mighty now to have a go at turning the spit for me?" Dummy turned the spit with a happy heart.

THE BIG CARVED CHAIR, almost a throne, was set for Robin at the center of the table. The Men sat in order of seniority—not of age, but the length of time they had been with Robin. Dummy, naturally, sat at the end of the table, with Thomas and Jehan.

At first, as the threescore Men all wearing Lincoln green took their seats in the Pleasaunce, Dummy felt very shy. He had never met so many of them before, since usually most of them were away on missions decreed by Robin. They were of all ages from very old, white-bearded and bent, to mere boys. Some were tall and handsome, some small and gnarled. They were dark and fair, gentlemen and peasants. All of them, as Dummy knew from Marian, had one thing in common. Robin and his Men had saved them from the cruelty and greed of Prince John or his followers, and, like Robin, they were sworn to see that justice was done. Some had had their lands stolen, their wives and children taken from them. Others had been condemned to death and escaped, with Robin's help, or had suffered cruel punishments. One man had had his ears sliced off, another had lost his bow fingers. One, luckier than many, had been saved by Robin from blinding with hot irons.

As they took their places at the table, Robin said a long grace to Our Lady of the Forest, and then they sang the song of the Men.

> In summer the greenwood shines so fair
> We make our home in the leafy wood
> We live in the faith of Christ our Lord
> Under the rule of Robin Hood.

In winter the wind blows bleak and cold
Our fingers are nipped by snow and frost
Yet still we take from the greedy rich
To succor the poor and save the lost.

It was the tune Dummy had tried so hard to play on his pipes and had only just mastered.

The Feast began with a cameline brewet, pieces of meat in a cinnamon sauce. The mead went around, and Robin's Men drank deep of it. Then they tucked into the roast swan, poached from the Bishop of Hereford's lake by one of the Men, as well as venison, and lampreys, tiny fish that tasted delicious. While the Men ate the marzipan and sweet pies, Robin, who had sat laughing with John and Marian, stood up. He was a slim, dignified young figure, wearing on this occasion not the famous green but a cloak of Lincoln red, a wonderful deep crimson.

"Some of the Men wondered whether we should hold the Long Day Feast this year, knowing as we do that our days here may be numbered," he began. "And it is true that our enemies are moving against us. But even if this is to be the last such Feast in the Forest, I wanted us to be together tonight. Life in the greenwood teaches us to live each day as it is given to us, and our trust is, as always, in Our Lady of the Forest." Dummy felt the deep silence as each man thought of the dangers the coming year might bring.

"The first toast, as you know, is always the same," Robin went on. "It is to our sovereign lord, His Majesty King Richard, Richard Coeur de Lion, wherever he may be now. May God keep him safe and bring him back to us, to end the tyranny of Prince John."

"Our sovereign lord, King Richard," repeated the Men gravely.

This solemn moment over, Robin smiled with pleasure and held up his goblet once more. "To the Men," he said, "and to the Woman"—he bowed to Marian—"of the greenwood, who fear no tyrant, who allow no injustice, whose task is to take from the rich and give to the poor."

"To Robin's Men and the Woman," they chanted, "who take from the rich and give to the poor." Their voices were deep and strong.

Dummy never forgot the effect of threescore men and one woman all standing, making their solemn promises. At that moment he knew that, whatever the danger, he longed to be one of the Men himself.

Finally, as the evening darkened, and the setting sun touched the tips of the oak trees, the Men gathered around a huge fire at one end of the glade. As the mead jug again went around the circle, they took turns to entertain. Some sang love songs and riddle songs, others told jokes or stories. Dummy had been up early that morning and he could scarcely keep his eyes open, but he was enjoying himself so much that he did not want to miss anything. As he strained forward to see whose turn it was to sing next, he heard the voice of Robin.

"One present Our Lord has brought us this year in the greenwood has been our new friend, Bird. We shall keep you and cherish you, Bird, until you are big and strong, and then you shall choose where you would like to live. In the meantime . . . some of us have heard you play the song of the Merry Men very beautifully on the pipes that Will made you, and we would ask you now to play it for us."

Dummy was suddenly terror-stricken. Although he knew that there was a rule that everyone must entertain, he had not realized that it included him— he thought he was too insignificant to count. But, in this company, Robin's word was law.

With shaking fingers Dummy lifted the pipes that hung at his belt and drew a deep breath. Then, nervously, rather jerkily, he began to play the notes that he had played so often and so confidently.

At first all went well and the notes were pure and accurate. But then, suddenly, he felt the silence and the eyes of all the Men upon him. He saw Marian looking at him with that doubting look he had learned to dread, and at that moment the tune began to go badly wrong. The pipes slipped from his fingers, his lower lip began to tremble, and he was so afraid he was going to cry, there, before them all, that he got up and rushed from the table. He stumbled blindly along the lantern path back to the Trystell Tree, wanting only to seek refuge in the darkness where no one could see his shame. He threw himself down on the ground among the trees and sobbed.

Suddenly all his troubles overwhelmed him—his old terror of Master, his pain at not being able to speak, the feeling that Marian did not like or trust him and that he did not after all belong anywhere. Maybe, since he could not even do his part to entertain at dinner, Robin would send him away. He heard a distant laugh from the Feast and thought they were all probably laughing at him.

As Dummy's tears subsided he knew that there was something he wanted, needed, to do, and at first he could not think what it was. Since he had come to the greenwood and hidden his stick in the Trystell Tree, he had rarely scratched out his secret sign. He had been too happy to need to do it, but now he was very unhappy.

He made his way through the darkness to the Trystell Tree and reached up into the branches for his stick. He grasped its comforting knobbly end and pulled it down. Then, in the light from one of the lanterns, he began to scratch the signs upon the ground and was comforted to discover that he still remembered how. He formed the upright stick with the circle and the tail, then the straight upright sign, then the circle that was not complete. He was just finishing the last bit of the sign, completely absorbed in what he was doing, when Jehan's voice said, "Bird, we missed you."

He spoke to him kindly, but Dummy was so startled that he could think only, as he used to think with Master, of not letting him see his secret. He sprang to his feet, and with his shoe began desperately to try to erase the signs in the dust. But he had carved them deep and for a long moment they stood there plain for Jehan to see.

"Richard!" Jehan spelled out, and the sound of the name said in his clear, strong voice transfixed Dummy. Memories suddenly flew up out of an inner darkness and he stood staring blankly at Jehan, scarcely aware of what he was doing.

There was a long silence.

"I did not know you could write," Jehan said at last. Dummy shook his head.

"But you have written something on the ground," said Jehan gently. "You have written a name: Richard."

There was another long pause as Dummy searched Jehan's face to make sure he had not misunderstood.

"I wonder . . . is it . . . could it be that it is *your* name?"

Then Dummy knew, and with the knowledge came the memory of the fair woman in the pretty, warm room who had ruffled his hair, and, yes, had shown him how to make these signs on a wax tablet with a silver stylus. She had done many other things with him too. She had cuddled him and kissed him, had told him stories and sung to him, had sat with him at the table as they ate delicious food, and had tucked him into bed. She had never hit him.

Sometimes they were together inside a big house, much bigger than Master's, with fine carpets and silver and pictures. Sometimes they went out into a garden with clipped hedges and flowers. Often they had been with a big, bearded man who had picked Dummy up and carried him. Once he remembered the man sitting him on a stone lion in the garden and saying, "You're a brave boy. Not afraid of the lion." Lions he felt were important— there had been pictures of them on a flag on the wall. . . .

What was it that had happened so that one day he was in that beautiful house and the next in the squalor of the farm, where everyone always seemed to be angry with him? In some part of him he thought that he knew. Why did he not dare to remember?

Jehan's question echoed in his ears, and slowly, his eyes full of tears, Dummy nodded at him.

"Richard," Jehan said again, slowly, thoughtfully. "You wrote it, and you told me," Jehan said gently. Dummy nodded again, suddenly feeling proud that he had done it.

"About the playing," Jehan went on awkwardly. "It has been a long day—it *is* the Long Day, after all—and we knew you were tired. Don't feel bad. We all make fools of ourselves sometimes. And don't stop playing the pipes. We like to hear you."

Again Dummy searched Jehan's face, wondering if he was laughing at him. But Jehan looked back so frankly and freely that Dummy knew he spoke the truth.

"You shot well," Jehan went on. "I can't think how you learned so quickly. We must shoot together—I am lazy about practicing. And about everything else!" He laughed happily, and Dummy had the feeling that, in a way he did not understand, the incident with the stick had made Jehan his friend. Tired as he was, he could not sleep, thinking partly of Jehan, partly of the life to which the name Richard was the clue.

EIGHT

Robin in Danger

THE LONG DAY was the beginning of high summer in the Forest, traditionally a time of peace and idleness for the Men. They sat around on the mosses by the Trystell Tree, or on the clipped sward of the Pleasaunce, telling jokes or stories, teasing, laughing, sleeping, listening to Dummy play. In the long hot afternoons, they took the chance to mend their clothes, to carve, to select pieces of yew to make new bows for themselves, to trim and feather arrows.

In the warm, short nights everyone slept in the Pleasaunce, and Dummy loved to lie watching the stars through the branches of the Trystell Tree, or enjoying the soft wash of moonlight upon leaf and branch. He found himself lulled to sleep by the soft *churr*ing of the nightjar, and the peaceful hooting of owls. When he woke in the early dawn, the Forest seemed fresh and alive as if the night had bathed it clean, and he would slip out of the Domain to go for a walk or a ride. Once, because of Master's teaching, he had been afraid of the Forest, but now he was at home in it and knew parts of it as intimately as he knew Robin's Country itself. It was a kingdom of slender white birches and massive oaks, of bramble and bracken, of swaying tawny grasses that waved in hidden fields in the heart of the Forest, of small hillocks and rough crags. Nesting in its secret places were boars and wolves, which he had learned would not attack him unless he threatened them, myriads of squirrels and shrews and mice. He came to be on nodding acquaintance with a charcoal-burner, an old man who lived in a hut in the Forest, making charcoal out of old wood, and with old women who grazed their sheep and pigs on the margins of Sherwood. He liked best to lie on the sandy floor of the Forest gazing up into the branches and the blue sky beyond through the stippled, shivering leaves of a birch, and he found a happiness in being alone. He loved the company of the Men, but he also needed this private space to think his thoughts alone.

Robin, he observed, also needed time on his own. He spent much time sitting, or kneeling, alone in the Oratory, and when Dummy was sent to fetch him to a meal he often found him very still and quiet, as if caught up in the strange green stillness of the Forest.

One day Robin announced that he intended to go to Mass at St. Mary's Abbey.

"I have not been to Mass for too long. Our Lady is missing me. I will go tomorrow."

Dummy could feel Marian's sudden quick anxiety. "But to St. Mary's? The High Cellarer might recognize you. There are many churches where you might attend Mass. Why put yourself in danger?"

Robin gave his boyish grin. "Perhaps I like the danger," he said. Knowing that Robin despised the rich monks of St. Mary's who dined sumptuously while the poor starved, Dummy thought Robin also enjoyed teasing the monks. Then Robin added, "I will take Bird with me to keep me out of trouble."

Marian frowned. She had not liked the way Robin had taken to choosing Dummy as his companion, and Dummy felt hurt at her continued distrust of him.

It was so hard to be under suspicion yet never be able to defend himself, and harder still to have to live with Marian's coldness. He longed for her good opinion, but even his shooting at the Long Day Feast had brought nothing but a cool "You've got a lot to learn." At least Robin seemed to have stopped suspecting him.

THE ABBEY CHURCH OF ST. MARY'S was built of gray stone, and Dummy liked its bare, simple arches. The altar, however, was dressed with expensive lace and with rich gold vessels and candlesticks, and the procession of monks approaching the altar wore cloth of gold, such as a king wears, and cloaks embroidered with jewels. Yet the monks claimed to be poor.

The church was very crowded, and Robin and Dummy stood at the back, Robin with his face in shadow beneath his hood. Dummy, who had felt anxious at this public occasion, knowing that the Abbot of St. Mary's was an old enemy of Robin's, began to feel safer, just because they seemed so well hidden in the crowd. Yet, when the crowd diminished a little, Robin moved forward to where he had a better view of the altar, and Dummy realized that they stood in full sight of the monks who were singing in their stalls in the chancel.

After a bit Dummy noticed the eye of one of the monks turned in their direction. Soon afterward the monk left his stall and went away—perhaps to tell the Abbot of Robin Hood's presence—and when he returned he again glanced surreptitiously in their direction. Dummy squeezed Robin's hand to indicate his alarm, and in response Robin took his and moved away backward through the crowd, making for the west door. Dummy felt very relieved to see the square outside, empty except for a peddler, and even better when they had left it and turned away down a side lane that led to the country, though he noticed the peddler, who had packed up his things, easing himself along with his crutch in the distance.

They walked on. Robin, who liked to go to Mass, was lighthearted and full of jokes. Dummy would have loved to ask Robin why he took such risks.

As he had done so often since the day of the Long Feast, Dummy felt in his pocket to enjoy the feel of his silver sixpence. This time he was upset to discover that it did not seem to be there. Immediately he turned around to see whether he had dropped it, and his heart contracted with fright. For there, only a few feet away, his eyes fixed upon Robin's back, was a man with a knife in his hand.

"Robin!" The name rang out in a cracked voice, and Dummy was too frightened to be surprised that the sound came from his own lips. Robin swung around, and with an instant reaction prepared himself for the onslaught of the man with the knife. Dummy looked on unbelievingly as the two of them swayed and struggled, Robin holding the wrist of the man with the knife, fighting to keep it from his own breast. The man with the knife slipped and the two of them fell to the ground, both struggling for their lives.

Terrified, Dummy saw blood pouring from between them and thought for a long, terrible moment that Robin had been killed, but then Robin stood up, himself white and shaken, and said, "I have killed him, Bird. I had no choice." He held out his arms and Dummy went to him and hid his face in Robin's jerkin, overcome with the horror of the attack and the death.

"You saved me, Bird, you know that?" said Robin. "You saved my life. And more than that, you *spoke*."

Dummy looked up, trying to see whether he

could speak again. He imagined a sentence—"Robin, I was frightened"—but, as usual, no words came.

Seeing this struggle Robin said, "Don't worry if you cannot do it again at once. You *can* speak, that's what matters. Gradually it will come back to you."

When the first shock was over, Dummy helped Robin carry the man, whom he recognized as the peddler, into a nearby barn, averting his face from the blood and the horrible wound. There was a plow in the corner, and Robin placed the body behind it where it could not be seen.

"It will take them a little while to find him, and by then we'll be far away," said Robin, his face full of pain. "I wonder if he has a wife, children, who will miss him and mourn him. Go on your journey, friend. At least you do not have my death on your conscience."

Robin slipped off a cross he wore under his shirt and placed it in the man's fingers, and he made the sign of the cross over him. "God forgive you," he said.

"The Abbot and I have been enemies for years," Robin told Dummy. "I have no doubt that it was he who paid this man to follow me and try to kill me. God will understand the poverty that drove this man to it, but he will not forgive the Abbot who paid him." Then he stood for a while, apparently praying.

Dummy was longing to get away, to return to Sherwood Forest and safety. If he could have spoken—and he did try—he would have said to Robin, "Let's go." But he stood as dumbly as ever, frightened and angry.

The trip back to Robin's Country felt long and weary. Both of them were silent and sad, Robin because of having killed his attacker, Dummy because of the fight, the blood, and the sight of the dead man. If he had not turned just when he did, it might have been Robin. He remembered, with a spurt of exhilaration, the way Robin's name had been forced out of him. Yet it was also frustrating. He *could* speak, yet somehow he still did not understand the trick of it.

Robin did his best to cheer him. "Only another mile, Bird. Supper should be nearly ready." He laid his arm affectionately around Dummy's shoulders. "I'll never forget what you did for me today."

But Dummy felt too sad to care about supper and as soon as they got back he disappeared to the underground bedchamber and climbed into his bed, pulling the blankets over his head. He heard the Men outside laughing and singing and the smell of stew drifted down to him. Suddenly he heard Marian very softly calling his name. He pushed the blanket off his face to find her sitting on the ground beside him, looking at him with a kindness she had never shown him before.

"Bird, I have come to say I am sorry. Robin told

me how you saved him, how brave and good you were. I can never thank you enough." Dummy gazed blankly at her.

"I haven't always been very nice to you," continued Marian. "I was so afraid you had been sent here to trap Robin."

Dummy longed to be able to say "It doesn't matter now," but instead he shook his head gently from side to side.

"There's something else too. Robin told me you had spoken, had called out his name. It did not surprise me. I already knew that you *could* speak—I have heard you calling out in dreams, you see. One day you will find you can talk like other people, I am quite sure. Something or somebody has frightened you very badly in the past."

By the time Marian left him, having brought him a plate of chicken stew, Dummy felt much more cheerful. He *did* belong here, he would learn to shoot as well as any of them, even as well as Marian herself, and he would grow up to be Robin's faithful man. He suddenly realized that he no longer felt afraid that somehow Master would get hold of him again—he knew that neither Robin nor Marian would let him go. His last waking thought was *This is my home now*.

NINE

The Bishop of Hereford

BEING FRIENDS WITH MARIAN changed everything. Now she laughed and talked with Dummy just as she did with the others. She suggested to Much that it was time to start making him a suit of Lincoln green, and she sat beside him at meals. His shooting lessons were transformed too. Many of the Men had told him that he had a natural ability as an archer, but feeling that his teacher was no longer harshly critical of him sped his progress.

"You *have* worked hard, Bird," she said.

One day when he shot particularly well—he was conscious of getting everything right, of being both relaxed and concentrated, of forgetting himself yet feeling fully himself—she came over and kissed him.

"That's our Bird!" she said, and he glowed with pleasure at his success. But he felt no more able to speak than he had been before, and that was painful.

More and more, as he got stronger and felt the Men loved and appreciated him, he longed to join in their talk and their jokes. His silence shut him out and this made him sad. But he did like the open way Marian now talked to him.

"Robin makes such enemies," she said to him one day. "When he thinks men do bad things, his method is to tease them publicly, to shame them in the hope they will change their ways. But they don't change—they come to hate him more and more and to thirst for revenge. Gradually his enemies are joining together, seeking Prince John's help, and one day, if he is not careful, they will try to destroy him. *I* keep telling him, Little John keeps telling him, but you might as well tell the wind."

Dummy could not help agreeing with her, but he thought Robin loved danger, and loved the fun of his teasing, too well to change his ways. Robin had given up any hope of a normal life when he came to live in the Forest, so now he flirted with danger and perhaps with death. No wonder Marian, who loved him so much, felt afraid for him.

He remembered this conversation with Marian a week later, when Robin outlined a plan he had for teasing the Bishop of Hereford. Robin had publicly mocked the Bishop many times for his grand house, his expensively dressed servants, his ermine capes, his costly clothes of silk and lace, his rings set with huge jewels. Robin also mocked him for his greed— for the huge dinners he held night after night with every sort of exotic sweetmeat and for the enormous quantities of wine he drank.

"The cost of one of the Bishop's dinners," Robin said, "would feed the poor of Hereford for a month!" He then made up a song about it with a lilting, jolly tune, which everyone sang in the streets of Hereford.

The Bishop writhed under Robin's mockery, and, like the Sheriff, he swore to take revenge. But he was frightened of Robin too, and when he needed to ride near to Sherwood he often put off his Bishop's clothes and dressed himself like a merchant. This was foolish—Robin was just as likely to stop a rich merchant as a bishop—but the Bishop was too proud to do the one thing that might have saved him, to dress himself and his servants in the simple garments of poor people.

So it was that on one hot August morning the Bishop was riding along a road near to the Forest on his huge black horse—the only one in the stable big enough to hold him—wearing a russet suit with a large plumed hat. His three servants wore plain gray livery. The Bishop was going hunting, with his falcon on his wrist. Beneath his gloves he was wearing two of his enormous rings, one with a great ruby stone and one with an emerald.

When he saw a poor old woman, some shepherds, and a little shepherd boy sitting around a fire by the roadside cooking some meat, he reined in his horse. He was hungry, which always made him bad-tempered, and the smell of the meat, as it roasted, was so delicious that he knew he could not wait any longer for a meal.

"Old woman, give me a piece of your meat!" he said sharply to the old woman.

"Sir, we are poor people, and we scarcely ever eat meat," she said timidly in reply. "There is not enough for us as it is."

"Do not argue, woman!" said the Bishop. "Unless you give me that piece of meat you are roasting over the fire, it will be the worse for you, I can tell you."

Looking near to tears, the old woman handed the Bishop's servant the stick with the meat beautifully roasted upon the end of it. The Bishop was so eager to taste the meat that he kept trying to pick it up while it was still too hot, but in the end it was cool enough to eat, and the Bishop took a generous bite from it. For a moment he was silent as he enjoyed the taste, and then suddenly he spluttered with rage.

"Venison!" he exploded. "You are eating the king's deer!"

"We were starving, sir," said one of the shepherds.

"I'll have you hanged for this!" said the Bishop, red in the face. "Tortured and hanged! You know how Prince John treats villains like you."

"But it is King Richard who is our king," said the old woman in a strangely defiant tone of voice.

"Arrest them, all of them!" said the Bishop to his servants. "Bind their hands."

"Even the child?" asked one of the servants.

"Of course," said the Bishop.

Dummy fought his fear. He knew that Robin Hood had carefully planned everything. The old woman took out a bugle from beneath her skirt and blew three blasts upon it. Before the Bishop's servants could bind anyone's hands there was a rustle in the undergrowth and twenty young men in Lincoln green emerged, their bows at the ready. They were soon followed by twenty more.

"It is time to remove disguises," said the old woman, pulling off a wig to reveal the ruddy hair of Robin Hood. A few moments later he had removed skirt and shawl and stood before them in his usual suit of green. He waited for a moment, as if expecting the Bishop to say something, but he stood silent, apparently both fearful and raging.

"It is well known that I hate to dine alone," said Robin, "and plainly you are hungry, sir. A plump merchant always makes a good dinner companion, so may I invite you and your men to follow me? But first, may I know your name?"

After a painful hesitation, the Bishop said that his name was Nicholas—Nicholas of Clipstone.

"A neighbor!" said Robin.

The Bishop looked frightened as one of the Men grasped his horse's bridle and another blindfolded him. His servants also looked wretched as they too were blindfolded, obviously fearful that the afternoon would result in their deaths. A strong outlaw held the bridle of each of their horses, as they plunged deeper and deeper into the Forest, through thickets and undergrowth and sudden wide clearings. At length they arrived at Robin's Country and led the Bishop through the Thicket and out into the Pleasaunce. When they removed his blindfold he looked around him in astonishment, more particularly when he saw the tables laid for a feast.

"You see that I was in earnest when I invited you to dinner," said Robin. "Bring Master Nicholas water to wash!"

Dummy fetched a basin of rose-scented water and knelt before the guest in the custom of great houses. Dummy could see that the Bishop was troubled, and hesitated to remove his gloves in order to wash his hands.

Eventually, he took off his gloves, and with all eyes upon his beringed fingers he bathed his hands, before Robin conveyed him to the seat of honor beside his own great chair at the table.

"Although we are rogues here," said Robin, "we never sit down to eat without giving thanks to God. Might you know a prayer to grace our humble meal?"

The Bishop mumbled a prayer, as if unfamiliar with the words, and Robin thanked him and offered him the delicacy of a tiny pastry filled with beef marrow. For once the Bishop had little appetite.

When dinner was over, Robin turned to the Bishop and spoke.

"Nicholas, it has been good to have your company, though you are a silent man. Is something on your mind? As you are among friends, I wonder if you would like to unburden yourself."

The Bishop shook his head. "I thank you for the dinner, sir, but now I must be on my way."

"I think not," said Robin. "I think not. In the first place, you must give thanks for your dinner, in the time-honored manner of guests, by offering us some entertainment. But that is not all. Perhaps because we have little of this world's goods, God has conferred a special grace upon us. It is to recognize a priest wherever we see one, however he is disguised. We do not know what modesty drives you to conceal your holy orders, but we beg you not to be grudging with them here. Poor rogues and outcasts as we are, we do not often have a chance to hear Mass. We must beg you, therefore, to stay with us overnight, to hear our confessions, and to say Mass for us in the morning when we take Communion fasting."

"M-Mass?" stammered the Bishop.

"Indeed, Nicholas," said Robin, holding up the hand with the Bishop's ring upon it and then ostentatiously kissing the ring in the manner that people kissed the ring of bishops.

"First, however, we will hear from Jehan, who took the liberty of looking in your saddlebags while you ate. Tell us, Jehan, what did you and Bird find there?"

"Three hundred gold pieces, master."

"That is a lot of money," said Robin thoughtfully.

"It is to be distributed in charity," said the Bishop hastily.

"In that case," said Robin, "trouble yourself about the matter no further. We will ourselves carry out your kind intention by distributing the money among the poor."

The Bishop turned pale. He looked as if he wished to speak, but then thought better of it.

"But there is a more urgent matter," continued Robin. "Before you hear our confessions, we believe *you* have a confession to make to us. Not only can we recognize a priest in disguise but we can also recognize a bishop masquerading as a merchant. Why are you disguised as Nicholas of Clipstone? Could it be that you fear punishment for your misdeeds? There are, after all, many poor people in the diocese of Hereford, and it seems to me that you have added to their burdens when you should have relieved them. You have tithed and taxed your tenants, you have been a hard man, and merciless in punishment, we hear. Could it not be that it is now your turn to be punished?"

The Bishop shook his head so vehemently that his jowls trembled. "I am a man of Holy Church, and you will be excommunicated if you lay a finger on me," he said.

"Dear me!" said Robin. "Excommunication, is it? An ugly threat. Well, not until you have said Mass for us at least! Then what? What shall we do with you after you have said Mass for us? What do you think, Little John?"

"Cut off his head, little master," said Little John promptly. The Bishop looked green with terror, and his eyes filled with tears.

"Pardon," said the Bishop. "I ask your pardon. Tell me your reckoning and I will pay it."

"It is wondrous high," said Robin. "Tell me, where is your purse?" Fumbling, half crying, the Bishop drew his fat purse from inside his clothing and handed it to Robin. It was full of gold.

"Good," said Robin. "This will keep us in bread and ale until winter sets in. As we eat and drink we shall say a kindly prayer for you. However, it seems to me that if there is to be reparation for all your unkindnesses to the poor, we shall need more money than that. Those fine rings you wear on your fingers, they must be worth a great deal. Think of the widows who could have warm blankets, the orphans who might have shoes and coats, the old who might have food in their stomachs if those rich jewels were sold. In Christian charity, my lord, now that I have put the kind thought into your head, I know you will wish to give up your rings."

Very slowly and reluctantly the Bishop drew the rings off his fingers—he had loved to see them sparkling and winking in the light.

"Then there is your falcon," Robin Hood went

on. "A fine falcon, trained by your lordship's own falconer, would be worth a great deal, would he not? We shall be glad to sell him for you, and give the money to the poor for the good of your soul." The Bishop shook his head and turned paler than ever. He loved the falcon, which was the best hawk he had ever owned.

"Since the Bishop is so generous, Little John, I think we must be merciful. We shall forgive him his faults and allow him to keep his head on his shoulders if he provides some entertainment for us as we digest our dinner. What do you say, Bishop, will you dance for us?"

The Bishop shook his head unbelievingly. "I never dance," he said.

"Nonsense," said Robin. "You are too modest. In any case, it is better to dance on the solid earth than at the end of a rope, is it not? Yes, I thought you would see my point."

So, while Will Stutely played his lute, and Dummy his pipes, the Bishop, scarlet with embarrassment and rage, pointed his toes and twirled about. To begin with Will played slowly—a stately minuet—but gradually he sped his playing until the Bishop was obliged to perform a fast jig and he collapsed purple-faced and panting on the ground. Dummy felt rather sorry for the Bishop, but reflected that the Bishop had caused much more unhappiness than the Men were inflicting on him this night. He remembered the hungry children he had met in Robin's company.

"Yes, well, not a very polished performance," said Robin. "Though doubtless you would improve with practice."

The Bishop got no sleep that night, for he had to listen to the confessions of each of the outlaws, one by one, and he suspected they were making them unnecessarily long. But however much he yawned, there was always another man waiting to take his turn. When he had finished hearing the confessions it was time to say Mass, which he did wearily and tearfully, passionately longing to be far away from Sherwood Forest and the outlaws.

"Very well," said Robin at last. "The Bishop has danced for us and said Mass for us, and now we must not keep him any longer. Put him on his horse, Little John, and send the horse off in the direction of Hereford." Little John lifted the Bishop bodily into the saddle, facing the horse's tail, tied his feet beneath the horse, and gave the horse a slap on the rump that sent him galloping off through the trees. That was the last they saw of the Bishop.

"As to the Bishop's men," said Robin, "we shall blindfold them and escort them part of the way home. After that they are free to make their own way, though we shall keep their horses. Good day, gentlemen, we have enjoyed your company. And now," Robin continued, "let us take the Bishop's gold pieces and give them to those whom he has wronged in the past. Bird, come with me and we will ride toward Newstead. Little John, you can take the eastern road."

Only Marian seemed unhappy about the incident. "Why do you need to make such enemies?" Dummy heard her ask Robin next day. "The Bishop will seek his revenge, that's certain."

Dummy listened with interest to what Robin would say to that.

Robin laughed. "I can't resist teasing," he replied.

TEN

The Shooting
Contest

"RICHARD, WAKE UP. Thomas and I are going fishing at the Secret Lake." Without opening his eyes, Dummy knew that it was Jehan who called him. He shook the sleep out of his eyes and climbed joyfully out of his bed.

Thomas was putting pasties and raw onions into a bag, and Jehan was already down at the Meadow saddling the horses. Generously the others let Dummy ride Star, his favorite horse. Jehan took a lean and rather bad-tempered gray for which, alone among the Men, he had a soft spot, and Thomas rode the palfrey that they had taken from the Bishop's men.

It was a hot day with no wind. Early as it was, it seemed stifling in the Forest. The flies bothered them all, and Dummy got tired of waving them away from his hot, sweating face. The Secret Lake seemed farther away than he had remembered. But suddenly Jehan turned off a barely trodden track between the trees onto another path overgrown with bramble and meadowsweet. And all at once there was the Lake, cool and shining before them. Jehan was already tearing off his jacket and breeches, and in a few moments he had dived headlong into the still water. Thomas was only just behind him.

Dummy had not expected this and did not quite know what to do. Running through his mind was the thought that such a lake was familiar to him. Somehow he knew what you did when the ground was no longer between your feet, how you trusted yourself to the water and it held you up. So he followed Thomas, and was soon half falling, half diving into the water. He fell downward into depths so cold that it made him gasp, then came up, his eyes blinded until he shook the water out. And then, immediately, he began to swim with bold, confident strokes.

He had never been permitted the leisure to swim at Farmer Jordan's, and in any case the brook was not deep enough to do more than paddle, so how did he know how to do it? Suddenly, sweetly, but disturbingly, he remembered a male face looking encouragingly at him in just such a pool as this one, and the struggles of his smaller self to reach the man, with splashy, excited strokes.

Dummy swam on, out, out, into the center of the Lake, his mind racing. He thought of a word—"Father"—that seemed to reverberate in his mind, even in his mouth. Had he said it out loud? He had a feeling that perhaps he had, but when he made an effort to do so no sound came. There was an odd kind of struggle going on inside him, as a memory of something painful jostled with good memories of the man's arms holding him, tossing him in the air, supporting him as he began to swim. "Father"—the word came again, and again he did not know whether he had said it or merely thought it. There was a kind of peace and joy in the idea.

He floated on his back and gazed up at the blue sky full of light, with tiny cirrus clouds like a flock of lambs. He had always known that Farmer Jordan and his wife were like a blot on a page that had once been clear. They made it hard to trust life, hard to feel that something or someone was not going to hurt you and keep on hurting, yet he did trust life, just as he trusted the water to hold him up when he swam. He trusted the kindness and goodness of Robin and Marian and Little John. He trusted Jehan.

He turned at that moment and saw that Jehan was only a few strokes behind him, his curly hair plastered to his head by the water, but his eyes looking at Dummy with the friendly, laughing look that was typical of him. And then suddenly Dummy could feel the word bubbling up from inside him, as a few minutes before he had felt the word "Father," only this time it was unstoppable, it came right out of Dummy in a clear, recognizable sound.

"Jehan!" he said.

Jehan stopped swimming, and a look of delight passed across his face.

"*Richard!*" he said, and for a moment they held each other's gaze, smiling as they noted the extraordinary thing that had just happened.

"Can you do it again?" Jehan asked. Dummy suddenly felt frightened, and he guessed that Jehan saw his fear. He turned and swam back to shore as hard as he could. Suppose he could *never* do it again, so that if Jehan told Thomas or the Men they might think he was pretending, not being honest with them? It was troubling. But Jehan said nothing to Thomas and behaved just as usual.

They ate their pasties ravenously and drank water from the spring that fed the Lake. Then Thomas showed Dummy how to lay his bait, and they sat there through the long sleepy afternoon on a high bit of bank. Dummy dozed a little—it had been an early start—and woke to the perfect silence of the hidden place, with only birdcalls disturbing its silence. He did not catch a fish, though Jehan caught a grayling.

In the late afternoon, tired and warm, they rode slowly home to Tucky's supper. Over the meal Jehan and Thomas told Robin about the day, but perhaps because of the mute appeal in Dummy's eyes Jehan said nothing of the moment in the Lake. Dummy felt very grateful to him.

The next day Dummy sat with Robin and Marian in the Solar, a small green space surrounded by hedges.

"The Sheriff is holding a great shooting contest at Corpus Christi," Robin told Marian, "and the first prize will be an arrow with a shaft of silver and a head and feathers of beaten gold. The contest is being cried in Nottingham and in all the local towns and villages so that many will compete."

There was a long moment of silence, and Dummy was aware of Marian's eyes searching Robin's face. He avoided her glance.

"I myself will try for this fine arrow," said Robin, "with the best of my marksmen—Gilbert, Little John, Scathlok, Reynold Grenelefe. And you yourself, Marian, if you have a mind to it, my love," he added, his eyes alight with mischief.

"It's a trap, Robin," exclaimed Marian. "You must see that. The Sheriff knows that you won't be able to resist competing, that you will be the man who wins, and he will arrest you and get his revenge."

"But that is what makes it so exciting," said Robin. "Don't you see? The pleasure will be in outwitting the Sheriff!"

"When he knows what you look like, and how well you shoot? No disguise can change that."

"We shall see," Robin said evenly. "It is the difficulty of it that makes it fun to wear disguise. The Men will hide in the crowd, also disguised, so that if the Sheriff tries to arrest me they can stop it at once. I shall be perfectly safe. And I shall have the pleasure of teasing the Sheriff once more."

"You will do as you wish," Marian said shortly, turning her head away. Dummy saw a tear on her cheek.

"Quite so," said Robin.

Dummy, along with the other outlaws, worked out his disguise. Robin found him a velvet suit that someone had given him, a suit that must once have belonged to a child from a rich family. He wore the velvet with a silk shirt and a hat with a plume. The feeling of silk and velvet next to his skin felt delightful, and also familiar, as if once before he had dressed like this.

Marian wore the neat, sober clothes of an apprentice in his holiday outfit. Her dark hair was tucked into a cap. She looked exactly like a boy who is nearly a man. Little John wore a sailor's trousers and jerkin, while Will Scathlok wore the dark green uniform of a verderer, one of the king's foresters. Much, as rashly daring as Robin, wore his old miller's clothes, still white with flour. Gilbert dressed as a knight, and Reynold and Jehan as squires. When the day of the contest came, Dummy set off on the walk to Nottingham with Marian and Gilbert. He realized that he had not seen Robin and had no idea what disguise he wore. Robin, Little John, and Will Stutely had taken horses, he knew, so that when the contest was over Robin could leave Nottingham quickly. Gilbert and Dummy were excited, but Marian was silent and pale, probably full of foreboding, Dummy thought. He took his place in the crowd, glad to see Thomas, Will Stutely, and other Men among the onlookers. The contestants stood in an enclosure to one side of the field. He could see Marian and Gilbert, and Little John had joined them in his blue sailor clothes. As yet there was no sign of Robin.

At one end of the field sat the Sheriff and his lady on high seats to give them a good view, and Dummy thought that if anything the Sheriff looked fatter than he had that day in the square. Almost at once Dummy perceived that the Sheriff was nervous and that he was scanning the contestants repeatedly, searching, he had no doubt, for the face of Robin Hood. On a table below the Sheriff, glittering in the sunlight, was the silver arrow with its head of beaten gold.

The time for the contest to begin was announced, and the archers came forward three at a time to try their skill. Some could not even hit near to the target and the crowd laughed and jeered at them, as they turned away crestfallen. These were mainly farmers' boys with clumsy bows they had fashioned themselves with little skill. In this preliminary stage the Sheriff, Dummy noticed, drummed on the arm of his chair with impatient fingers.

Gradually the number of contestants became fewer. Among those who shot well was a tall red-haired man, at least a head taller than Robin, his fine looks marred by a long scar. Will Scathlok discharged every shot perfectly, hitting the target squarely. Marian, slim and graceful in her boy's outfit, did equally well. Another contestant who showed surprising skill was an old man who wore a red and yellow patched coat, almost like a clown, with a patch over one eye. Voices mocked him unmercifully: "Can you see the bow, Grandpa?" "Where's your cap and bells?" "Where's your monkey?" they cried, but he silenced them with his accurate shooting.

Where was Robin, thought Dummy. Unless he arrived soon, only Will and Marian would carry the honor of the Men. Dummy wondered whether someone had warned Robin, or whether, far worse, he had been seen and captured on the way to Nottingham.

Eventually the four outstanding contestants stood alone. There was a break while the Sheriff and his lady retired to take a midday meal, and the poorer people around the field munched their bread and cheese. Dummy made his way to Marian, his fears for Robin uppermost in his mind.

When he reached her side she smiled at him, guessing his question as she so often did. "Don't worry," she said. "For the moment he is quite safe. Truly. And for the rest, we must leave it to Our Lady to protect him."

Dummy nodded. He tried to convey to her, in dumb language, what a wonderful shot she was.

"And a good teacher," she answered. "Which means that you too will be a fine shot. If you practice every day."

Dummy hung his head a little, because life had been so interesting in the Forest recently that he had not found much time to practice.

At a sign from the Sheriff, trumpeters played to signal the beginning of the most exciting part of the contest. The butts had been moved a considerable distance. This would be a real test of marksmanship.

The Sheriff, Dummy noticed, now sat well forward in his chair, his eyes eagerly fixed on the contestants. He was studying the tall red-haired stranger attentively as if he thought he might actually be Robin.

Only if Robin has grown three handspans, Dummy thought, *and even Robin cannot change his height.*

Will shot first. Two of his arrows reached the outer ring of the target and the third reached the inner ring. Then the tall man shot, a perfect shot right in the center of the target. A shout of admiration went up from the crowd. Then he shot again, less perfectly, the point of his arrow on the circle rim of the bull's-eye. His third shot split his first arrow in half. Dummy noticed the Sheriff whisper to one of his servants, and two men in the Sheriff's livery moved close to the red-haired stranger, perhaps preparing to arrest him. The Sheriff would soon find out his mistake, Dummy thought.

Will now did less well, failing to get any of his arrows into the target.

Marian sent all three arrows to the center of the

target, and the onlookers went wild with excitement.

The old man in yellow and red limped forward. "Beat that, Grandpa!" someone shouted. Of course, nobody could have beaten it because it was a near perfect performance, but the old man matched Marian by sending three arrows unerringly into the bull's-eye, each one splitting the one before it.

"Holy Mother of God," sighed someone in the crowd. "It's a miracle."

It was not the way the old man walked, still less the way he looked, that gave the game away to Dummy, but suddenly as he watched the old man shoot, realization dawned. But surely if he could recognize Robin, then the Sheriff might do so too. Dummy watched carefully and saw that the Sheriff had lost all interest in the old man and in the contest. His eyes were fixed upon the red-haired stranger.

Finally, only Marian and the old man stood up before the crowd. By this time the target had been moved four yards farther away, a distance at which few bowmen could shoot with accuracy. The contestants were anxiously surveying the new distance. The old man threw some remark to Marian and Dummy longed to know what it was.

Marian shot first. Her first shot hit the outer rim of the target, the second hit the middle, and only the third reached the inner ring. People in the crowd sighed and murmured.

Now all eyes were on the pitiful old man, who

plucked his beard nervously and did not look as if he had the strength to shoot so far. His first arrow came fast and strong from his bow and struck the circle of the inner ring. The second arrow found its place midway between the circle and the center. The third arrow was in the bulls'-eye itself. The cheers were loud. In a fit of excitement some of the crowd picked the old man up and carried him at shoulder height up to the Sheriff to receive his prize.

The Sheriff, who had set up this expensive contest for one purpose only—to catch Robin Hood—gave away the silver arrow cheerfully, with all his thoughts concentrated on the red-haired man his servants were already hustling away through the crowd. The old man bowed low when he received his prize and limped painfully away into the crowd. The crowd dispersed.

Dummy walked happily home with Marian, her hair free of its cap, her boy's clothes bundled under her arm. And there, outside the Thicket, was the old man limping up and down in his red and yellow coat, holding the precious arrow in his hand. He came up to Marian, kissed her lovingly on the cheek and said, in a voice impossible to mistake for any other, "Told you so, didn't I? A lovely tease. One the Sheriff will never forget."

"But he doesn't know it was you," she objected.

"He will!" said Robin. "Oh, he will! I'm not finished yet. Sit down and help me write a poem."

"A poem?" said Marian, puzzled.

"Yes. Now, how should it go?

Come from Sherwood's leafy wood
Your old acquaintance Robin Hood
In feeble likeness of the old
He won the prize of beaten gold.

"Not great poetry, I admit, but I think he'll get the idea."

"You are sending it to him?" asked Marian, wondering who the messenger would be.

"Better than that," said Robin. "I am giving it to him myself!"

Only later did Dummy and Marian learn what Robin had meant. That evening he set off for Nottingham once more, still carrying his bow, but wearing his Lincoln green suit.

As the Sheriff sat at dinner in his Great Hall, an arrow flew through the open casement and landed quivering in the opposite wall. The Sheriff turned pale.

"There's something attached to the arrow," said his servant, pulling the shaft from the wall. He carried the paper to the Sheriff's wife, who read Robin's poem aloud to the whole company.

"Get him!" the Sheriff shouted. "Send out a posse of armed men. I want Robin Hood alive or dead." But although the Sheriff's men immediately clattered down the stairs, buckling on their sword belts and helmets, by the time they reached the street the square was empty. Robin had vanished back into Sherwood Forest.

Fall

ELEVEN

The First Battle

IT WAS A FINE AUTUMN. Day after day the sky was a deep blue, and the sun glinted on the bronze leaves till the Forest was full of brilliant light.

The Men went about their business as usual and yet . . . something was very different. Since the dinner with the Bishop of Hereford and the shooting contest, Dummy had become aware of a growing tension in Robin's Country, of some danger that threatened them. Marian's face was often grave these days, and Dummy took notice of the many conversations between her and Robin that broke off as he approached. He longed to ask just what the danger was.

Yet outwardly all was the same. Marian gave him shooting lessons every day and he practiced assiduously, partly to please her, partly because he had come to love the pleasure of shooting for its own sake. She was still as strict as ever over detail.

"Your feet are *quite wrong*," she would call out suddenly, or "What are you thinking about? This takes *all* your concentration."

On one unforgettable day, it suddenly seemed to Dummy that the bow was now so familiar that he scarcely knew where it ended and he began. As he shot, it felt like letting a part of himself fly free. The arrow went straight and true to the heart of the target, and he had never shot so far before.

"That's our own Bird," said Marian. "Now you are really one of the Men." He felt very pleased with himself.

Dummy had a secret from Marian, in fact from everyone except Jehan. Just occasionally, when he was out alone with Jehan, he would find a word speaking itself. Once he said "Good" in reply to a comment of his friend's. On another day he said "Hot!" The words went smoothly across his tongue as if they had escaped beneath some grim portcullis and glided over a drawbridge unnoticed.

It was important to him that, apart from a gentle smile, Jehan made no comment. And Dummy knew now, from experience, that Jehan would not speak of it to others. Yet he knew also that Jehan rejoiced for him.

It was odd: he had no more control over the words than he had ever had; it was just that, now and then, they had learned to say themselves. And as he spoke more, he noticed that he played his pipes less. They were ceasing to be his voice.

Life felt good to him in other ways too that autumn. He was still very close to Robin, and he took part in many of his adventures. As always, life with Robin was exciting and surprising. One day, when Dummy was out with Robin and the Men, they heard a barking of orders and a clinking of chains and suddenly a long line of prisoners came into view, guarded by soldiers wearing the uniform of the Sheriff's men.

"They've not been prisoners long," said Robin as they watched, hidden in the trees. "They're still wearing their own clothes and they don't look like skeletons. But they shan't be prisoners much longer."

Following Robin's lead, the Men overpowered the guards and tied them up, took their keys and released the prisoners. They brought them back to Robin's Country, fed them, and heard their pitiful stories. As always, Dummy felt very proud to be among the Men.

Sometimes, particularly on bright, sunny days, Dummy visited the Secret Lake, not only to swim but to watch its still surface with the trees hanging upside down in it and to see the pattern break when the wind blew across it.

One day, as he left the quiet circle of the pool, he felt a tremor of alarm, though he saw nothing to frighten him. Almost at once he identified what it was: a slight trembling of the ground. Just as he thought he was imagining it, there it was again. It was the sort of shaking, he thought, that might be caused by many men and horses passing through the Forest.

He stood very still, trying to work out the direction of the movement, and then he thought that, far away, he heard a bugle. It seemed to him that many men must be moving somewhere to his right. That was good, because the bracken would give him cover for a long distance, and he ran, with the light, loping run he had learned in the Forest and with the newfound strength that the food and the life of the Men had given him, toward the sound and the movement.

He was running slightly uphill, and the path, he knew, came out on a rise from which it was possible to look down onto a grassy plain below. Panting now, he came to the lip of the rise and leaned over.

There, many feet below, drawn up in companies, were several hundred men with horses, each company with its group of archers. As Dummy watched, other men were marching and wheeling into place, and he guessed that they were poised there waiting till other companies arrived. He had little doubt that this small army sought to find and destroy Robin and his Men.

He could see men in the Sheriff's green and yellow livery struggling beneath a heavy litter that almost certainly carried their fat master. On a big black horse, wearing armor, sat another man. Dummy was sure it was the Bishop of Hereford. From the plain where they stood, Dummy knew that the soldiers could make their way directly to Robin's Country, but only, of course, if they knew its whereabouts.

Just at that moment Dummy noticed a thin figure, who looked vaguely familiar, gesticulating in the direction of Robin's Country. With a sinking of the heart, he recognized the man as one of the chained prisoners they had helped. Marian had thought that Dummy was a spy, but here, it seemed, recently disguised as a prisoner, was the true spy.

Dummy ran back to the lake, where he had left Star. He leapt upon his back and rode as fast as he could back to the Domain. Star, picking up some of his panic, galloped gracefully beneath him. If that army burst upon the Men unawares, they would all be killed. If they had warning . . . Dummy did not know what difference it would make, but he knew that they must have the chance to escape or to fight back.

Slipping down from Star and throwing his reins over a branch in the Thicket, Dummy ran, his legs trembling, until he reached the Tree. There he gave a cry, a mixture of a shout and a croak, that no one had ever heard from him before. In a moment Robin had a steadying arm around Dummy's shoulders and was giving him all his attention.

Desperate to communicate, yet painfully far from speech, Dummy grabbed up a stick and in the earth beneath the Trystell Tree tried to draw what he had seen. He drew a soldier, then pointed in the direction of the army.

Robin reacted immediately. "Just a few soldiers?" Dummy shook his head. "An army?" Dummy nodded, and Robin looked grave. "Still some distance away?" Dummy nodded again.

Robin turned to Will Stutely. "Will, take the

fastest horse in the Meadow, go with Bird and get him to show you what he has seen. Then come straight back."

Then Robin lifted his horn and sounded it.

Men began to tumble out of the Hideaway, from the Pleasaunce, and the Oratory and the Forest beyond. Soon they were joined by others from the Field of Practice. In a few brief words Robin described what Dummy had seen and the danger in which they all stood.

"We have one advantage," he went on. "Thanks to Bird we are expecting them, whereas they imagine they will be taking us by surprise. We shall put up a good fight. We can guard our entrances well, and they will not easily overrun us. The worst danger, as you all know, is that we could be besieged here in the Forest, and they could starve us into submission." Robin's voice faltered briefly, but that was the only time he showed any emotion about their plight.

"God keep and bless you all," he went on. "We have been brave and merry, good friends and companions. We have laughed and feasted and sung, and been on many adventures together. If we can be victorious here in the Forest we will enjoy many more such times. If we should die together, I know of no gentlemen in whose company I would sooner die. Let what will be, be, and let us conduct ourselves with high courage and with faith in God. There is love and trust between us—the best of friendship and comradeship. It will make us fine soldiers.

"One last thing—before you all go to your places, don't forget that if I am killed or injured, Marian is my second-in-command. You will take your orders from her." Marian nodded. "Meanwhile, let it be as God wills." Then, like the intelligent leader he was, Robin at once sent each man to his place, reminding him of his duties. He sent the strongest men to roll huge rocks to block the inside of the Thicket entrance and placed men inside the perimeter to shoot at any who attempted to struggle through it. He sent Thomas and Oswald up to the topmost branches of the Trystell Tree to report what they could see from that high perspective.

"Gilbert, I put you in charge of the Ravine. Go to the caves on this side of it. Take six men and be prepared to repel anyone who tries to climb. Arm yourselves with boulders, spears, oil, as well as arrows. Jehan, I want you to act as runner between the Ravine and the Trystell Tree, where I shall be standing. You must keep me informed about what is happening there, and take my news back to Gilbert. How are our food supplies, Tucky?"

"Good," said the friar cheerfully. "We can hold out for weeks."

"Work out each man's daily ration so that he is not hungry but has no more than he needs. Before that, however, give every man a measure of mead to drink before battle begins."

By the time Will returned with the saddled palfrey, the whole Domain was in the process of preparing for war.

Dummy galloped ahead of Will and soon they came to the rise where he had watched the massing army. He slipped off Star and, followed by Will, went forward to the edge of the hillside. He had a sudden mad idea that he might have imagined the whole thing and that the plain would be empty, but the men were still waiting, and others had joined them.

Will whistled gently. "I must try and count them," he said softly, and Dummy could hear him telling off the tally on his fingers.

By the time the two of them returned to the Domain, there was a very different feel there. Each man had taken his appointed place and prepared himself for battle. Tucky was handing around the mead that Robin had ordered—a goblet for each man.

"BIRD," SAID ROBIN, after he had had time to confer with Will, "I want you to keep our archers supplied with arrows. You will need to collect them from the armory and then run to each of the archers in turn. It is a tiring job, but very important."

Dummy was delighted that Robin had given him a proper job to do. He went to the armory to roll out the wooden barrels in which the prepared arrows were kept. There were many of them, but all the same he wondered what would happen when all of them were gone.

Gradually the whole Domain became silent. It was now midmorning, and though it was not hot, the Men wiped away sweat and became edgy with the tension of waiting.

Marian, in her boy's clothing, sat astride a fallen treetrunk near the Trystell Tree, her eyes fixed upon Robin, who stood perfectly still, waiting. He looked at her, smiling the smile Dummy had noticed before whenever he was in danger, as if he were living entirely in that moment of time without thought for past or future, and was thoroughly enjoying himself.

The waiting seemed to go on for a long time, but finally first Much and then Dirk, whom Robin had sent out as spies, rushed up to Robin.

"They're coming, master. They'll be here by noon."

Soon Thomas, high in the Trystell Tree, came slithering down.

"There's about fifty bowmen, master. They've set them in a half circle outside the Thicket."

"Very good," said Robin, and gave the order to his own bowmen to loose their first shots. The arrows fell thickly on the unsuspecting army outside the Thicket, and there were cries and screams that showed the arrows had hit home.

At the same time Jehan arrived from the Ravine.

"They're trying to climb it," he reported, "but my father's keeping them at bay. He said to tell you no one will get through."

For several hours the soldiers tried in vain to enter the Thicket, but while they struggled with the boulders and the dense mass of thorns, the Men easily picked them off, and gradually they drew back to consider new tactics.

In their relative safety behind the Thicket none of the Men was hurt. Running to and fro with bundles of arrows, wiping the sweat from his eyes, Dummy felt as if the battle would never end, but in the late afternoon a bugle sounded, there was shouting on the path beyond the Thicket, and then, at last, an eerie silence. The Men looked at one another and grinned. They had survived the first round.

Robin climbed to the Ravine to talk to Gilbert, and was glad to find that all was well there. Gilbert was in the act of pouring a stream of oil down onto the stones below to make them even more slippery. One of the Men had been wounded slightly by a stone, and Robin sent him down to be tended by Tucky, who had set up a sort of field hospital in the Pleasaunce. He told the others to rest while they could, and he promised them food and drink within the hour.

The Men ate their supper and then tried to rest, all of them sleeping on the sward aboveground with bows beside them, and many with swords as well. Tucky had lit a fire, and Marian and Robin sat beside it, not attempting to sleep. Dummy dozed beside Marian, refusing her suggestion that he should sleep snug in the Hideaway. He woke, stiff and bitterly cold, in the dawn, and heard the ominous sound of the enemy bugle.

TWELVE

The Long Wait

THE SECOND DAY OF BATTLE was like the first. The soldiers attempted to storm the Thicket, but were beaten off by the skill of Robin's archers. One or two of the Men were slightly hurt, but as the watchers in the Trystell Tree knew well, a number of the Sheriff's men and the Bishop's soldiers had been seriously wounded, and some of them had even been killed.

"They won't continue with this," Marian said to Dummy. "Why should they, when they could starve us out?"

Her words were prophetic. The next morning, although soldiers were on watch a safe distance away from the Thicket, there was no attack. That day was a relief to the Men. They spent it making new arrows, devising new methods of defense, taking turns to sleep, and enjoying their rations, though Tucky was now giving them out rather meagerly.

But then several days passed in uneasy quiet, and the atmosphere inside the Domain became a little strained. Robin's Men were used to roaming far and wide in the Forest, hunting, riding, and running; and for so many of them to be cooped up without activity made everyone nervous. The Domain began to feel less like a home than a prison.

To counteract the boredom, Robin proposed long hours of shooting practice, with rewards for those who shot best. Fortunately, the October days were sunny, and the evenings, though chilly, could still be spent sitting around a fire, with songs and stories to while away the hours.

After a week of this enforced idleness Robin called a meeting of the Men.

"As I see it, there are two possibilities," he told them. "One is that, rather than lose more men, they have decided to starve us out. I have consulted with Tucky, and with care we could make our stocks last till Christmas, though we shall need to cut down on our rations considerably. The other possibility is that the Sheriff and the Bishop have alerted Prince John and that they are waiting for him to send engines of war. The Prince, if he chose to help them, could doubtless supply scaling ladders and platforms, battering equipment and slingshots. Against such devices we could not last very long."

Looking at the circle of grave faces Dummy felt a sudden pang of fear.

"I am proposing to send out a spy," Robin went on, "to try to find out their plans. As you know, the only way out of the Domain apart from the Thicket is to climb along the side of the Ravine. After dark, and it would have to be after dark, that is no easy path. And the job of spy is a dangerous one in any case. I am therefore asking for volunteers."

So many of the Men stepped forward that Robin laughed. "Perhaps we should all go," he said lightly. "Will Stutely, I choose you. Come aside with me, and we will discuss your method and your disguise."

THAT NIGHT Dummy dreamed of a giant battering ram pointing at him and finally coming straight for him. He woke in a sweat of fear and found that Tucky was also awake.

"Bad dream?" asked the friar sympathetically.

Dummy nodded. With the memory of the dream still vivid, he felt terrified.

"It's a scary business, being attacked," Tucky went on. "Particularly when you're young and you've got a lot of life ahead of you. If we could smuggle you out, perhaps you could go to a family in the village till the fighting is over?"

Dummy struggled with himself. To his shame he longed to be out of this dangerous place—somewhere where he could eat and sleep and play without fear of dying. On the other hand, he *was* an outlaw, or he had liked to believe so when things were going better. These people were his friends and his companions, and to leave them the moment they were in trouble seemed a strange thing to do when they had nursed him back to health and given him a home.

He shook his head.

Tucky had noted the silent struggle Dummy was having with himself and smiled. "None of us would think the worse of you," Tucky said. "You are young yet. But if you *do* decide to stay, then you must do as we do. That is, trust. First of all, trust Robin and Marian. They are good commanders. But if they fail to deliver us, and anyone may fail, then trust God. Trust whatever may happen to you. All of us are afraid of pain," Tucky went on. "And rightly so. But when the moment comes, then we have only to deal with the one death assigned to us. There's not much point in imagining many different sorts of death."

Dummy realized that that was just what he had been doing.

I do want to live, he thought, surprised at how fervently he wanted it. Back in the dark days at Farmer Jordan's there had not been much to live for, but it was as if Robin's Country had shown him how good life could be.

"We have to be generous with our lives," Tucky went on, "as with everything else."

Robin, Dummy reflected, had given him an example of living generously, caring for others in Prince John's England where so many were brutal and greedy. Suddenly, as he remembered Robin, Dummy felt stronger. The longing to escape had left him.

"One day," Tucky continued, "you may look on these days of the siege as one of the most important things that ever happened in your life, even if, just now, you would give something to be safely out of it all."

THE NEXT MORNING Dummy felt fresh from sleep and ready to give himself to the day ahead.

It was as slow and tedious as the previous days. For the first time the weather had turned cold—there was a rime of frost on the trees and a glaze of ice on the tiny pond in the Meadow. Tucky had further reduced the rations. Used to the generous food of the Domain, it was hard for Dummy to have to tighten his belt on a mere slice of bread for breakfast.

When Will returned, some days later, Dummy was starting to remember the old familiar sensation of hunger. The Men were shorter-tempered and less high-spirited.

Robin called the Men together, and Will told them what he had discovered.

"I went first to Nottingham to see what I could hear there," he began. "The Sheriff is in a rare temper against you, but as soon as he let it be known that he was trying to raise troops to fight Robin Hood, the people would not help him. They are on your side, of that there is no doubt. But I could discover nothing there of battle plans.

"At Hereford I had a piece of luck. There is a monk there, a good fellow who was once at school with me. I sought him out, asked a question or two, and discovered he did not care for the Bishop.

" 'Did you know the Bishop has a monk as his secretary?' he asked me. 'It just so happens that that monk is from my very own cloister.'

"After talking to the monk, my schoolfellow came with news of letters exchanged between the Bishop and Prince John. It appears Prince John has promised that, in another month, he will move soldiers and equipment to Mansfield, and from Mansfield he will come here to join the attack."

"Good," said Robin. "So we know when the attack will come, and also how long our stocks of food must last."

This news did not seem to Dummy to be particularly good, and his feelings of dread returned.

That evening Robin repeated Tucky's question to him. "What would you feel if we could get you out of here, Bird?"

This time Dummy had his answer ready, and he shook his head at once.

It occurred to him that being with Robin was like being the vassal of a lord, and he wished that he might promise to serve Robin all his days in the way that vassals did, kneeling with his hands between Robin's. Robin gave one of the smiles that had become rarer as the days had gone by.

"You're a brave boy. Since you see yourself as one of the Men, then I accept you as one, no longer a boy but a man."

WINTER

THIRTEEN

The Siege

THE LONG DAYS OF THE SIEGE went slowly by. It was bitterly cold, and it needed all Robin's ingenuity to devise games and exercises to keep his Men warm and fit. Fencing and wrestling passed the time, but it meant that they all came to supper with huge appetites, and the stew with its meager share of vegetables and meat did little to appease their hunger. Dummy noticed, however, that whereas in the earlier days of the siege they had been short-tempered with one another, exasperated by confinement, now, knowing the danger that awaited them, they seemed gentler, kinder. When they sang together the songs were old, sad tales of love and battle, and when they prayed with Tucky in the Oratory their voices deepened with feeling. Every one of them knew that at the end of their present ordeal they faced probable death or imprisonment. There were jokes and laughter, as there had always been, but it was the laughter now of courage, not of bubbling high spirits.

Dummy had never admired Robin and Marian more. They seemed always to know who was frightened, who was losing heart, and to be beside them, encouraging, consoling, cheering. He reflected with surprise that, cold and hungry as he now often was, this was in some ways the best time he had ever had with the outlaws. There was such a sense of fellowship, of brave resolve.

"If we must die," said Robin, "then we die together with our honor intact. Throughout Prince John's reign, we have fought for justice, cared for the poor, and righted wrongs, as is the command of Our Lord Jesus whom we serve and His Mother whom we revere."

Finally, there arrived the long-awaited news that Prince John's men were camped at Mansfield, less than a day's march away from the Forest.

Seeing the set faces of the Men, and Robin's exhausted face, it came to Dummy once more that they stood little chance of coming through the ordeal safely. Either they would be overcome and invaded by the soldiers, or they would be forced to stay within the Domain till they ran out of food and starved. Somehow he did not think Robin would surrender.

For a whole day nothing happened. Then, at last, in the late afternoon, their fears were realized. Soldiers in the black uniform of Prince John came to the Thicket with a battering ram and mounting platforms. They arranged them carefully in a semi-circle surrounding the Thicket, managing to get them into place despite the hail of arrows from Robin's Men. Watching from high in the Trystell Tree as the huge battering ram was wheeled to the edge of the Thicket, Dummy felt numb with despair. The Domain would be invaded and destroyed.

Suddenly, however, a youthful figure scrambled up the rock the Men had rolled into the entrance to the Thicket. Only partly shielded by the rock itself, the archer drew his bow and shot an arrow at the team of men working the battering ram. Nearer to them than any of the other Men, and high on his vantage point, he hit first one, then another of the enemy. Without their guidance, the battering ram rolled forward and struck the Thicket, tearing out a narrow passage within it, yet becoming entangled in thorn and undergrowth. Four of the soldiers ran after it, and the archer at once shot another of them. The wounded man reeled back out of sight. There was something in the brave bowman's style that told Dummy what he wanted to know. It was Jehan!

Dummy knew that he could not let his friend face such odds alone. Sliding down from the Tree, he snatched up his bow and quiver and ran like a hare toward the rock. He did not have Jehan's climbing agility, and at first he despaired of pulling himself up onto the ledge where he could stand beside his friend. But somehow he did it, and while Jehan leaned out to the right of the rock and loosed another arrow upon the men struggling to release the battering ram, Dummy edged his way leftward, peered out, and took careful aim. He pierced one of the enemy in his arm, and the man spun around with the pain, turning away from the machine. At this the others took fright, and, leaving the battering ram where it was, they turned and ran for cover.

Jehan grinned at Dummy.

"I think we've done it for the time being," he said. Dummy was proud of the "we."

It was growing dark now, and all seemed silent on the far side of the Thicket. Commending Jehan and Dummy for their bravery, Robin replaced them on the rock with older archers who, if there was a night attack, might have to shoot in the dark. Then he ordered supper and a rest for all who had fought so valiantly.

Tired by the long day, Dummy accepted Marian's suggestion of sleeping in the Hideaway. He woke in the middle of the night and got up at once. He was astonished to see that it had snowed, and the gleaming white cover lay upon everything. How he wished he was free to go out into the Forest, to see the beauty of snow on the branches and follow the tracks of the deer. Now it seemed unlikely he would ever again do such a thing.

He felt drawn to the peace of the Oratory and to his surprise found Jehan there, wrapped in his cloak, standing lost in thought.

He had never seen that merry face so serious.

"I am thinking of the men I killed today," said Jehan, "and others whom I injured." Dummy nodded. "But I thought of you too," Jehan continued. "And what a good friend you are to me. Let's always be friends."

Dummy smiled. For once no words were needed.

"About talking," Jehan went on. "Couldn't you risk it a bit more? Like on the rock today?"

Dummy hated his speechlessness to be mentioned, yet this was his friend Jehan, who really cared about him. He nodded, his eyes full of unshed tears, and turned away.

DAWN CAME and the weary Men once again braced themselves for attack. Soon a team of Prince John's soldiers were struggling again with the battering ram, this time trying to drag it out of the undergrowth of the Thicket where it was deeply embedded. Today Robin had two of his most experienced archers on the rock to make their task more difficult. Gilbert, Dummy knew, had beaten off two attacks from the Ravine. On the other side of the Thicket the soldiers had rigged up a platform from which they shot far into the Domain.

Dummy was aware, as he raced to and fro with arrows, that he was in continual danger. That afternoon Robin had given Jehan the job of watching from the Trystell Tree because he was the best lookout in the Domain, and many a time Dummy heard Jehan's voice ring out giving warning or advice. For the soldiers to come near enough to inflict injuries, they also had to come near enough to be seen by Jehan.

Suddenly, his back to the Tree, Dummy heard a cry and a thud, and before he turned he knew what he would see. There, lying on the snow beneath the Tree, lay Jehan, an arrow in his chest. He was alive, and even tried to smile, though Dummy could see the struggle with pain. Dummy took his hand, and forgetting his old fear he heard words move freely over his tongue.

"My friend, my friend, my friend . . . Jehan."

He sat there for several minutes, watching the snow grow red beneath his friend. There was a set look on Jehan's face that terrified Dummy. His eyes grew fixed and glazed, yet he struggled for speech. Bending low so that he could catch Jehan's words, Dummy heard and understood.

"Speak, Richard! Speak!" said Jehan. Then he closed his eyes and died.

IN THOSE TERRIBLE MOMENTS Dummy forgot all about danger and the battle; he came to himself eventually with a slow, dreadful awareness. There, no more than forty feet away, having somehow made his way through the Thicket, was one of Prince John's black-suited soldiers. He was not looking at Dummy, but was taking slow aim at someone beyond the Tree. Swinging around, Dummy saw who it was. Robin.

Perhaps the soldier knew it was Robin, and that

was why he took aim so carefully. Perhaps he was not trained as Robin's Men were trained, to shoot quickly and accurately. Either way, Dummy had slipped his bow from his shoulder, aimed an arrow, and loosed it before the stranger loosed his. It caught him full in his drawing arm, and with a cry he spun around and let his bow drop. The cry made Robin turn and in a glance he took in the scene. Jehan dead beneath the Trystell Tree, Dummy still holding his bow, and the soldier who had tried to kill him.

"So, young Bird, you have saved my life again," Robin said. For a moment Dummy stood speechless, and then, remembering what Jehan had said to him, he walked out upon the bridge of speech and said, in a dry, cracked voice, "Robin!" It took more courage than firing at the soldier. Robin took him in his arms and hugged him. Then Dummy began to cry. He wept bitterly for Jehan.

"Jehan was very brave," said Robin.

As usual the attackers drew away when it was dark. It was now terribly cold with the wind moaning softly over the snowy trees, and the Men warming themselves at several fires they had lit in different parts of the Domain.

WILL TRIED to dig a grave, but the ground was frozen so hard that he could not break the soil. So Gilbert wrapped Jehan in a cloak of Lincoln green and laid him tenderly in the Oratory, heaping the bright snow around him. He looked peaceful, a boy sleeping, ready to wake to a new day of work and laughter. It was so hard to know that Jehan would not wake on the morrow. Dummy felt as if he was carrying a stone where his heart was.

The next morning he felt that he cared little now whether he too would be lying in the Oratory by evening. Even the joy of saving Robin did not ease the pain of Jehan's death.

But though the sun rose on a beautiful snowy landscape, this time there was no attack. The day wore on and the Men looked anxiously at one another. What could the silence mean? Maybe another devastating attack of a kind they could not imagine?

Dummy longed to be alone, and he resorted first to his old nest in the Thicket, and later to the quiet of the Oratory. Eventually he climbed to Jehan's last seat in the Trystell Tree. From the topmost point, far away in the distance, he could see the tents of Prince John, in a clearing of the Forest.

He was hungry. Food was being shared out more and more sparingly as the days went by. In Dummy's hearing Tucky had suggested that the venison had hung long enough, that it was time to roast and eat it to give the Men one sumptuous supper, but Robin insisted, as before, that so fine a deer must be kept for a supper of celebration when the battle was over. Dummy could tell from Tucky's slight shrug that he doubted whether they would ever eat the venison.

Sitting up in the branches of the Tree, blowing on his cold fingers, Dummy saw what he thought must be a hallucination. A tall monk, his head half hidden in his cowl, stood outside the Thicket, waving a white handkerchief. He did not wave it like a man frightened or asking desperately for friendly treatment, but slightly scornfully, as if he was above asking for favors.

Suddenly Dummy realized that this was not a hallucination but a real monk, apparently alone. He could not see Dummy, who was well hidden in the Tree. With the instant response of his training, Dummy slid down to tell Robin of the coming of the stranger.

FOURTEEN

His Majesty

"A MONK!" Dummy croaked, pointing.

Robin strode through the Thicket, past his
guards. "Good morrow, stranger," Dummy heard
him say. "What brings you here? We have dined
monks here before, but none have come of their
own accord."

"I came in peace to dine with you, Robin Hood,"
said the monk, whose voice was deep, educated, and
self-assured. "I trust my flag"—he lifted the white
handkerchief briefly—"will give me safe passage in
this den of robbers."

"Came you alone?" asked Robin.

"No, I have a young companion," said the
stranger. "I do not want to put him in danger, but
I would be grateful if he might join me. He waits
outside in the Forest."

"Thomas, bid him come," said Robin. "Go
armed," he added softly, "and take Will with you.

Now, sir," he said pleasantly, turning to the stranger. "May we know your name?"

"You may," said the stranger, "but not yet. I will tell it to you over dinner. Or, better yet, you may guess it."

Robin frowned. He was used to a different reaction from his guests. There was something about this man that puzzled him. Plainly he had no fear of the outlaws, no sense that Robin's power might be a threat to him. He was a tall, handsome fellow, and he carried himself with dignity.

"Very well," said Robin. "Oswald, our guests will need to wash. See to it." Leaving his Men to bring rose water and a towel, to offer mead and soft seats beneath the Trystell Tree, Robin went off to confer with Tucky. Soon the delicious smell of roasting venison was wafting through Robin's Country. So Robin had softened his resolve after all, thought Dummy. Just as well. There was little meat left to eat, and this man was plainly accustomed to dining well. Dummy looked forward to the delicious dinner after the long days of privation.

Meanwhile Thomas returned with the stranger's companion, who, though only a boy, seemed as much a gentleman as the stranger himself. A pink-faced, fair-haired boy, he was about Dummy's own age and was smartly dressed in a brocade coat. The stranger introduced him as Hugh of Arncliffe, and the boy shyly took his place between Dummy and Thomas.

As they sat down to dine, the monk's cowl fell

back, revealing red hair and a long scar on the temple. Dummy at once knew where it was that he had seen him before. It was at the Sheriff's shooting contest. But monks did not shoot, nor did they carry the scars of battle. He could see from Robin's sidelong glance that he, too, had remembered the former meeting.

"Tell me," said the stranger. "What is the purpose of the band of Robin Hood? Is it to defy the law of the land, to rob, to spread terror?"

"Not at all, Brother," Robin replied. "You must be a stranger in these parts. We live in a country where the rich prey on the poor. The lords afflict their subjects with cruel taxes, lawful men are driven into exile, and cruel punishments are inflicted upon those who seek only to feed their hungry children. The monks, saving your presence, live lives of drunkenness and gluttony and forget the poverty they avow."

"You are quite right that I am a stranger here," said the monk. "And I do not like what I see. So what is it that causes such unhappiness? Is there not a lawful monarch who can impose justice upon lord and peasant and monk alike?"

"Alas, no, Brother," said Robin warmly. "Our true king, Richard, went to the Holy Land and has not returned. Some say he is a captive somewhere. In the meantime his brother John rules England and permits—no, rather encourages—the powerful and the greedy to commit acts of injustice."

There was a long silence while the visitor digested this information. When he spoke again, it seemed that he had changed the subject. "This venison is uncommonly good," he said pleasantly. "Tell me, do you yourself never break the law?"

Robin flushed a little. "We take the king's deer from time to time to remind ourselves that King Richard is a generous man who would not grudge us a good meal since we are his loyal servants."

"I see," said the monk. "That is well said."

They drank the usual toast to the king and to the Men, both of which the stranger drank with enthusiasm, and the Men sang the song Dummy loved. But still the stranger had not told them his identity. As Dummy watched him and listened to him he had the familiar feeling of groping for a memory, of trying to find his way back to that house where he had lived once with his mother and father.

Suddenly Robin turned to his guest. "We have dined you, Brother, and answered your questions, and now it is our turn to ask. Who are you, and what brings you here?"

"I will answer you," the monk replied in his clear, strong voice. "But first let me tell you that I fully share your grief about the state of England, and about the suffering of so many. I have myself lost dear friends under the cruel reign of Prince John. . . ." The voice was silent as if remembering. "When I heard of the life you live here, of your own small kingdom, I wanted to see for myself. As to who I am . . ."

The visitor held out a hand to the boy who had accompanied him, who left the table and moved to his side, bowing just before he reached him. "Robin, do you not know me? We were friends once, though I know that pain and imprisonment have changed me." The tall stranger rose from his chair, and Robin, staring at him, stood up beside him. "I am no monk, nor, it must be said, as good an archer as Robin Hood."

Robin and the stranger stared at each other as if transfixed.

"You are"—Robin's voice cracked in the surprise of recognition, and then went on—"you are . . . King Richard." At this all the Men rose to their feet, and Robin went down on his knees before the king. He held out his hands, palms together, and the king took them between his own.

"I am the true and faithful man," began Robin in a trembling voice, "of my king, my lord Richard, king of England. May God and Our Lady and the saints, whose relics lie in our Oratory, grant me their help; for to this end I shall devote and consecrate myself for the remainder of my life."

"So you promised me long since," said the king. "You have been faithful to your promise. On another occasion I shall give you my tokens, especially in returning to you your fiefdom of Locksley, but for now, rise, my good friend, and let us talk together like friends, not as king and subject."

So the king and Robin sat down with the Men and talked of all that had happened in the long years of Richard's absence. He spoke of his bitter imprisonment at Dürrenstein as he returned from the Crusades, of his rescue by his minstrel, and of how, when he returned, he resolved to come secretly into his kingdom to see how it fared. With this purpose he had traveled for some weeks in disguise. He had found sadness and suffering everywhere. Some of his oldest friends had been killed or imprisoned by Prince John, and when he had inquired for Robin of Locksley he learned that Robin was exiled in Sherwood Forest. Richard had come in search of Robin and discovered that he was besieged by his enemies. And at that moment the king had rallied his friends and supporters and reassumed his kingship.

"If it had not been so, I fear they would have overcome us," said Robin. "God has been good to us."

When the Men retired, Hugh, the page, made up a bed of bracken and heather for the king. But the king bade the boy use it himself.

King Richard and Robin drank together until far into the night. Dummy, who had gone to sleep exhausted in the Hideaway, woke in the small hours and felt that he would sleep no more. He stumbled out into the moonlight and was surprised to see Robin and the king sitting by the dying fire, still talking. He moved to join them, bowing shyly to the king, and he sat down at Robin's feet.

"This is Bird, also known as Richard," said

Robin. "Another Richard. Somehow he lost his family and came to join us in the Forest, and neither he nor we have ever regretted it."

Robin turned to look at Dummy, who had scrambled again to his feet and was staring at the king desperately as if trying to understand something. At first he could not speak at all, but stood sweating with the effort of expression.

"A l-lion," he stammered, his face red and his limbs trembling.

The king stared back at Dummy.

"A s-sil-ver cup," Dummy went on. The king looked as if he, too, was seeking to remember something.

"Your name is Richard," he said at last, "and you must be ten summers old? Just such an age as my godson Richard Walter, whose parents were taken and killed by Prince John for opposing him. Young Richard disappeared, whether killed or stolen away, no one knew. And yes, I gave my godson Richard a silver chalice with a lion carved upon it."

The king and the boy stared at each other, trying to take in what their encounter might mean. Then the king held out his arms to Dummy, and Dummy went to him, his eyes filling with tears as he realized that this man knew his parents and could tell him about them. The king embraced him with a great bear hug. After all these years Dummy at last knew who he was.

THE KING left the Domain next morning.

"I had sworn that Marian and I would not marry before Your Majesty returned," Robin said. "Now we shall marry in the spring, as soon as Lent is over, in Edwinstowe church, and if you please, Your Majesty shall give the bride away."

The king nodded. "Once you are married, Robin, I want you to serve me at court. I need men there whom I can trust, and I trust no one more than you."

Robin hesitated a moment, no doubt thinking that he was not a man for palaces and throne rooms. But he had made his vow to the king.

"Might I have one more summer in Sherwood?" he asked.

"Better than that," said the king. "In the autumn you shall leave the life of the greenwood and come to join me in London, but thereafter, if you wish, you shall return every summer to Sherwood, and sometimes I shall join you to forget the cares of court. And Richard here shall be my page till the day comes when he is as great a knight as his father before him. We have much to tell one another, he and I."

"To us he will always be our brave Bird," said Robin. "There will be a welcome for him in the greenwood whenever he comes to see us."

Dummy, who had once had no home and no family, now seemed to have two places where he would be at home, and one of them a palace. He smiled and spoke.

"I am lucky," he said haltingly.

MONICA FURLONG is the author of several noteworthy biographies of prominent spiritual figures, including Thomas Merton, Alan Watts, and Saint Thérèse de Lisieux, as well as the critically acclaimed young adult novels *Wise Child* and *Juniper*. Ms. Furlong lives in London.